Also by Ronni Sandroff

PARTY PARTY / GIRLFRIENDS

THIS IS A BORZOI BOOK
PUBLISHED IN NEW YORK BY ALFRED A. KNOPF

FIGHTING BACK

RONNI SANDROFF

FIGHTING BACK

ALFRED A. KNOPF · NEW YORK · 1978

THIS IS A BORZOI BOOK
PUBLISHED BY ALFRED A. KNOPF, INC.

 Published in the United States by Alfred A. Knopf, Inc., New York, and simultaneously in Canada by Random House of Canada Limited, Toronto. Distributed by Random House, Inc., New York.
Library of Congress Cataloging in Publication Data
Sandroff, Ronni.
Fighting back.
I. Title.
PZ4.S213Fi 1978 [PS3569.A5196] 813'.5'4 77-20372
ISBN 0-394-41310-5
Manufactured in the United States of America
First Edition

To my grandparents—

MOLLIE *and* LOUIS ALPERN

CELIA *and* WILLIAM SENDEROFF—

For their vision of a just society and their inability to leave well enough alone

FIGHTING BACK

1

Lizard flames, night sky, Father's warm neck. She was in her pajamas, curled against her father's chest, her head bumping his chin as he ran down the stairs. She could hear feet rumbling on the flights above them, voices calling out. Mother ran out the lobby door, holding the baby in a long blanket. Father started toward the door but a man put his arm out to stop them.

An orange flame leaped out of the dumbwaiter. Father's arm was across her face but she peeked under his sleeve to see the fire crackling against the wall. The heat made the air wavery. The flame bubbled the paint, smoking, then fell back into the dumbwaiter, leaving a few tickling fingers of fire on the wall. A man tried to push the dumbwaiter door closed with his jacket.

Father carried her out into the dark space between the buildings. The wind whipped papers around his slippered feet. It was the first time she had seen the night. She gazed up at the sky and her heart stopped at the beauty of the darkness after the orange flames.

A few days later they went back to the apartment to wait for the housing inspector. The rooms smelled of burnt coffee. Mother sat in a kitchen chair staring at the rubble. She picked Jeanie up and brushed the grit off her pants. The baby, Evan, had to stay in his playpen, which was melted a little on one side. Jeanie found a place in the wall where she could put her hand through and feel outside. Her chest bounced with joy. It was her fire. She could burn down buildings with the power of her heart.

A neighbor peered through the hatchet cuts in the door, then came in. "My, my," she said in a slow drawl, "what a pity. The fireman broke that beautiful set of wedding crystal you kept right there on top of the refrigerator."

"Huh? What are you talking about, Malvina?"

Jeanie hurried over to her mother. She had to listen carefully. No one ever told her anything. She had to find it all out by herself.

"Mister insurance is in the building, girl. Can't you remember 'bout your wedding crystal? You had to clean up the glass or the children would get cut."

"He'll never believe it," Mother laughed. "Where would I get wedding crystal? Whatever that is?"

"Didn't you ever read in the paper how those deb-u-tantes get china this and silver that and crystal glasses for their weddings?"

"Yeah, yeah. And they read about their less fortunate sisters living down here in the dangerous slums."

"Your rich cousin from New Jersey gave it to you, I remember. Let me think. It was one of those cut-glass decanters with a pointy little top. Ten matching glasses. A tray, too. Worth at least thirty dollars and never been used. Huh! I'm just waiting for the man to ask *me* what started that fire. I'll tell him what *I* know. Dragging children out in the middle of the night. Old lady from 5-F in the hospital. Landlord's in the building today, and he ain't crying."

"Think he set it?" Mother asked.

Malvina leaned against the sink, a hand on her hip. "You're supposed to be the communist, you tell me. Even if he didn't throw a match down, he set it. That dumbwaiter was so filthy. Nothing gets cleaned up around here."

Malvina's children were spilling into the hallway. Her muscular brown arm gave Mother's shoulder a little shake.

"So you be sure and remember 'bout that wedding crystal, honey. Hey, you kids, get in there."

Mother ruffled Jeanie's hair. "Malvina is wonderful," she said, "trying to pull something good out of the ashes."

Jeanie ran back to the place where she could put her hand through the wall and feel outside. Her heart burned with anger. The Hatchet Cut Landlord played with matches in the dumbwaiter and didn't care about the old lady in 5-F. The anger made her fall over on the floor it was so big. Big as the night sky with sirens ringing. She touched the ashen floorboard and wondered how you could pull something good out of the ashes. Like a magician pulling a row of scarves out of the hole in the wall. Mother picked Jeanie up and brushed the grit out of her hair.

2

Jeanie sat straight-backed in the hard plastic seat as the subway emerged from the underground. It was a new habit of hers, looking back, way back, as if her early memories contained a lesson she had missed, a principle she could use as a cane in the hours ahead. She sifted but could pull nothing more from the ashes. She glanced around the subway car. The old woman sitting next to her had her mouth creased shut, as if from a lifetime of keeping secrets. The other passengers focused their eyes on the middle space in the aisle. There were no drunks. No crazies searching for an open face. No Allees with gold discs on their shirts. As far as she could tell she was not being noticed.

Her thoughts rose slowly, like bubbles in a pot of water about to boil. She would make it home on time if the train didn't stall. She would embrace her daughter and wonder what that child's earliest memory would be. Perhaps today, tomorrow, would burn in her memory as the time her mother exposed her to the terrible commotion of publicity. The thought excited, rather than disturbed, Jeanie, who fingered her dark, tea-colored hair and leaned forward as if to impel the train faster into the future. She felt a pulse of energy. She was free of the nagging voice of inaction that had pursued her for almost a year. She had made her move. The Church of All might be powerful, but she was not alone.

The subway lurched, banging her back against the seat. For a moment the eyes of all the passengers met as they righted themselves, and Jeanie bent down to help the woman next to her pick up her shopping bag. It was 174th Street; Jeanie stood up to stare out of the paint-flecked window. She wanted to see it today. She deserved it. The train squealed slowly around an S-shaped curve: buildings, billboards, a street with traffic—there! For a brief moment the buildings parted and she saw water showering down ten feet of rocks. The waterfalls were framed by oak trees. The Bronx River stretched in an army-green curve below. Buildings, traffic. She loved that waterfall, though she had only seen it from the train. She continued gazing out at the low Bronx rooftops, imagining them planted with grass and bushes. She wondered how much topsoil would have to be laid over the tar roofs to grow a lawn, and whether the ceilings below could stand the weight. You're supposed to be the communist, you tell me. Was it inevitable that there'd be a lawn on every rooftop some day?

She remained standing, rocking on the handstrap, eager for her station now, for Leelannee's chatter, for a glimpse at the future she had opened up. As she stepped off the train, the wind cleared her mind of the rattling subway thoughts. She trotted down the stairs, her bright scarf flapping around the collar of her paratroop jacket.

Beneath the elevated train a man sat double parked in a dark-green Chrysler. He wove a thread in and out of the face of a baby deer on his needlepoint canvas. As he took a stitch he glanced at the street, saw Jeanette Burger striding from the station, and stabbed his knee with the needle. He slid the car into drive and cruised behind her, with the needlepoint still on his lap.

Jeanie climbed Lydig Avenue through a crowd of shoppers, finding refuge among the old people who hunched forward like ancient buffalo. Empty cartons narrowed the sidewalk to a single-file trail. She glanced at the prices in the small grocery window, noting they were a few pennies higher than the ones at Mirrormart, the giant market where she worked. At the top of the hill she set an empty crate next to the wall and tipped back into the false spring warmth of late January.

Moments later the wail of a small child made her open her eyes. "I want to go the other way!" he screamed as his mother tried to yank him in the right direction. Jeanie understood the mother's impatience, but she empathized with the child. She wanted to go the other way too!

What other way? Away from the future that blew cold on her neck, back under the fence and across the lot and down the hill to the park where she could rest under the tree that was about to fruit. When you grow up on the left the tree is always about to fruit. Jeanie tipped back the crate again and decided not to think about growing up on the left just now. She'd give herself a break. Grab two minutes of sunshine vitamin D.

Soon the school bus veered toward the corner, opening its doors before it quite stopped. As Jeanie sat up she noticed the dark-green Chrysler. Leelannee tripped down the steps loaded with a knapsack and lunch box. Jeanie took her arm, but stared across the street at the man in the Chrysler. The gold disc on his shirt burst before her eyes like a sunspot. With deliberate slowness she turned her back on him and lifted Leelannee onto the crate, tied her shoes, buttoned her coat, and traced the streak of dirt that looked like a line of tears on her cheek. Her back felt naked. But she couldn't let them scare her with ominous presence. She had come too far for that.

The child pulled on her, searching for attention. "Mommy. I have two notes for you. *Two* notes. They're very important. *Very*." She looked so intense that Jeanie smiled and took the clutch of colored papers from her hand. The avenue was one way. The Chrysler backed up a few feet, but the traffic forced him to a standstill. Jeanie hurried her daughter up the block. What did he mean by following her so openly? She would have liked to turn and try to make out his face, but she didn't want to provoke him.

"Can I buy a plant, Ma? Read it!"

Jeanie looked at the mimeographed notice about the school plant sale to celebrate an Israeli holiday.

"I want to buy two plants, Mommy. No, three plants! Okay?" The child flung out her arms and twirled up the block. The bright flower patterns on her jacket spun like a color wheel as she shouted: "It's springtime in Israel!"

Jeanie grabbed Leelannee's arm to keep her from colliding with a hydrant. The child's zeal for Israel annoyed her, but what did she expect sending her to that school? Don't worry. School values wash right out in the rain.

Among Leelannee's school papers she found the second note. It was handwritten on tinted stationery.

Your godship,

Please please please call. The number is 123-4567. Our lodestar is pulsing over your sphere. If not thwarted, the aspects are favorable. Do not resist the attraction. Please please please.

Faye

A wave of heat moved over her body. "Leelannee. Who gave you this note?"

The child hung on a gum machine, pleading.

"No, no gum, bad for your teeth." She wiggled her free of the globe that tottered in front of the candy store. "The note, Leelannee. Tell me who gave it to you." She led her across the street between parked cars.

"Mommy, can we go in the back way? Please."

"Fine. Tell me who gave you this note."

"You know who came to my school today? My daddy, Dennis. Tomorrow he's gonna take me for a long, long visit. You didn't tell me I was going to his house. He's gonna buy me a big, big coloring book and flowers. . . ."

"Did Dennis give you this note?" She almost said Brainstorm, the school nickname Dennis Blastrom had hated, the only tonic she'd been able to find for the seasick motion in her stomach that his name set off.

"It's very important, Mommy. I didn't lose it."

"Did Dennis give it to you?"

"Uh huh. Read it to me, Mommy."

Jeanie gazed down at the child as they swung in the back of the building. I love her crabapple cheeks and the way she falls over her feet when she walks. I'll kill Brainstorm if he tries to take her. Kill him with what? Lawsuits? Switchblades? Machine guns? He's got the whole church behind him.

She cast her face in a smile to meet the child's inquiring

look. On the way to the staircase she found herself poking her head into the laundry room to see if the lint had been cleaned off the exposed pipes. Gray webs stretched down in eerie clusters, brushing the top of her hair. "It's Halloween in there," she said to Leelannee. She needed a cleaner laundry room than this! The whole building could go up in flames.

"Come on, kid." Jeanie raced Lee up the stairs to the lobby floor. She turned her key in the smudged bronze mailbox. No mail. No mimeographed calls to coalition demonstrations. No bills. No pleas for contributions. No thinking until she was safely in the apartment.

Mrs. Feldman caught her as she was getting in the elevator. Jeanie tried to get off with a quick hello, but the woman held the door open. "I just rang your bell. Did you see downstairs?"

"I saw." Jeanie lifted Leelannee, who insisted on poking the broken elevator button.

"So? It's up to us again." Mrs. Feldman tilted her magenta-colored hair.

Jeanie sighed, her impatience slipping away for the moment as she confronted the old problem. She didn't know why most people refused to be active in the tenant's association, but she knew that those who were must act for all of them. She couldn't hold herself back. She slipped into commitments to the people around her. It was part of her background, her character. "I guess we should call another emergency meeting."

Mrs. Feldman nodded until Jeanie was afraid her bird's nest hairdo would topple over. "When should we make it?"

"Can you take care of it?" Jeanie asked. "Any day but Tuesday is good for me."

"Of course I can take care of it. You're always doing so much. You should get some rest, dear, you look tired. I don't know how you do it." She let the elevator door close and

Jeanie steadied herself on the railing. She didn't know how she did it either. The worse was not the shift at the supermarket, but the train ride home when she was always afraid the train would be late and Leelannee left standing in the street. Jeanie dug out her keys, clicked the locks, and pushed the door open as Leelannee rang the shrill bell. The gust of the door opening blew a white paper bag across the linoleum.

She flopped on the bed without taking off her paratroop jacket. Lee stretched out beside her, sucking her thumb with such intensity that her eyes almost crossed. Jeanie pulled the note from Faye out of her pocket and twirled it in her fingers. *Our lodestar is pulsing over your sphere.* Meaning they were in New York. Oh, those goddamned words which once slipped off my tongue like milk. *If not thwarted. . . . Please please please.* Only Faye could write such a sugary threat. Imagine if she just called her. Hi there, Faye, how's the new slavery going? Has the Church of All elevated Eli Zinger to godhead yet? How much do you pay the phone company to get a number like 123-4567? Yes, it is an easy number to remember. Say, do you think you could ask the heavy in the dark-green car to stop following me?

She stared at the ceiling, trying to gain control over her bubbling thoughts. The real question was, how did the Church of All find her so soon? Did All have some connection at the TV station? Or had they been looking for her since they came to New York? It could be that Faye just wanted to chat with her old confidante, that Dennis wanted to visit his child.

It was a comforting thought, but she had to admit it was unlikely. The sound of Leelannee's sucking was like the squeaking of a mouse. Jeanie gazed at the sleeping child, trying to think realistically. If she called Faye, Faye would control the conversation. That's what Faye was good at. So there was no question of calling, no matter how curious she was about how they had tracked her down. Brainstorm had found Leelannee's school; it didn't matter how. Jeanie sat up and struggled out of her jacket. She'd have to hide Lee until she was through with this thing. She'd keep her out of school, tuck her away somewhere far from the glare of publicity, somewhere Dennis Blastrom would never think of looking.

The decision relaxed her. For the moment they were both safe at home. She looked around her apartment with pleasure. A nest, put together with the bits of furniture her relatives discarded, yet reflecting the woman and child who lived there. A black and white abstract rug. Everyone commented on how unusual it was. A plush yellow lounge. A black fake-fur bedspread. All fabrics that pleased the touch. You could flop down anywhere. The window shade lying rolled next to the wall caught her eye. Imagine that Eli Zinger was once so poor he painted on window shades. When this was over she'd throw that out too.

She kicked her shoes off and lay down again, pulling the fur bedspread over herself and the child. She could hear the shouts of children in the courtyard and the radio next door. It made her rooms seem a little empty. She was still not used to living alone. It gave her too much time to think, not enough to listen. She was becoming introspective at thirty, a quality that had not cropped up in her life for years. She'd been displaced before, but that was in the tea-party atmosphere of a bigger family.

"When I first came to this country," Grandpa said. Jeanie banged her head scooting out from under the table. She liked stories that started like that. They were like stories about the beginning of the world.

Grandpa was resting his arms on the kitchen table. Aunt

Claire paused in the doorway in her smart shoulder-padded suit which had a flap for buttoning on a shoulder bag. Grandma sat at the edge of the kitchen stool. Mother turned from the stove where she was heating Evan's baby food.

"When I first came to this country," Grandpa said again, "Lasar, Avraam's son, went ahead and got me a pushcart to sell fruit on Delancey Street. In those days, thirty, forty, fifty pushcarts lined up along the curb. They had pots and pans, used clothes, everything. We were all in the pushcart union. Evelyn do you remember it at all? In the summertime it was hot—and noisy!"

Jeanie stood near Grandpa, watching him put a cube of sugar between his teeth and sip from his glass of tea. Since they'd moved in with Grandpa they spent all their time in the narrow kitchen eating, washing the dishes, drinking coffee, and starting all over again in a perpetual tea party.

"One day a car hit the pushcart way down on the corner and bump bump bump bump all the carts turned over, one after another."

Claire laughed and when Claire laughed Mother had to laugh too. Jeanie didn't laugh.

"I was knocked down under my cart right between the handles. I wasn't hurt. I started to get up, but Lasar yelled, 'Lay there, you greenhorn!' So I lay there with the oranges and the green bananas, and every time I tried to move out of a puddle Lasar said, 'Lay there! What do you know? This is not the old country. Lay there!' When the policeman came along Lasar gave him my name and address."

Grandpa laughed and wrinkles traveled up the smoothness of his bald head. "Lasar came over a year before I did, so he was a *mavan*. Two weeks later a man with a briefcase climbed five flights to see me and put fifty dollars in my hand. Fifty dollars in those days! Whenever anyone gives me money I am always able, ready, and willing to accept. Later I said, 'Lasar, what is this fifty dollars?' 'America, Shemuel, land of opportunity! Now you can rent a fruit stall.' "

They all laughed. Grandpa bit into the sugar again and finished his tea. Mother wouldn't let Jeanie do that. And she wouldn't let her pour a pool of salt on the side of the plate and dip food in the way Grandpa did. But she couldn't stop her from hearing all the stories and finding everything out for herself. Grandpa set down his tea glass, still laughing. "And the next year, when the crash came, and I lost my fruit stall, I went running down to Delancey Street. 'America? Lasar! Land of opportunity?' "

"Sam, let Evelyn finish," Grandma said.

Claire leaned against the door frame. "So you got thirty dollars from the insurance."

"A hundred and thirty all together," Mother said. "It will pay for the moving."

"But where are you going to find an apartment these days?"

"In Philadelphia," Jeanie said. They all laughed but it wasn't funny. Phil-a-del-phi-a. Like a long run down the piano keys. In Phil-a-del-phi-a things were different from here.

"Remember before the war?" Aunt Claire said. "The landlord would give us three months' free rent to move in. Them was the good old days."

Mother put Evan's food in the bowl with the circus animals around the edge. It used to be Jeanie's bowl. "Good old days? We moved every six months to get the free rent."

"And to avoid paying what we owed him." Aunt Claire lifted her face and laughed. It sounded like pouring water. Too loud.

"You know," Mother said, "we should have fought back like Jay's family did in Philadelphia."

Jeanie moved closer to her mother, getting right under her elbow. There were lots of different ways of fighting back. Ways to keep the tickling fingers of fire away from your door.

"During the depression they called the street he lived on Red Alley. They never managed to evict a family from that street. One time when the marshal was moving someone's furniture down the stairs, Sviete grabbed Jay and jumped into the van. 'Do you *know* how to drive?' she asked him. He was only ten, but you know Jay, he wouldn't admit he didn't. 'Yeah, sure I know, Ma. You turn this key here and one of these is the brake. Here's the clutch.' Sviete sat there trying to get the nerve up to drive the thing, then she said, 'You *sure* you have to turn this key?' 'Yeah, Ma.' 'You sure. Without this key it doesn't work?' '*Yeah,* Ma.' 'Jay, listen to me like a good boy. Take this key and go throw it down the sewer.' "

Jeanie stood with her hands on her hips watching them laugh. It wasn't funny. She wanted to get back to her own apartment with just Mommy and Evan and the radio all day long. All this tea partying and the stories that went round and round without ever coming to the end!

"Look at Jeanie," Claire said. "She looks just like Jay's mother now. Same blond hair. Same fire in her eyes."

"Would you let Evelyn finish?" said Grandma, getting off the stool to put the pots away.

"Oh," said Mother. "The point is that we've got an apartment. The city housing inspector said he never saw a worse looking slum. He wrote *burned out* and *emergency* all over our application, and Jay is a vet, so . . . We're moving into a new housing project, way up in the North Bronx."

"Where?" asked Grandpa rising in his chair. "Is that in the country? Does the subway go there?"

Claire came into the kitchen to hug Mother. Jeanie was

pushed out of the way by the sudden action of legs. She ran to the back bedroom mad mad mad. The big fire had to come and burn them down and they were never going back to the place where they lived, the apartment that had arms and legs and tangled Jeanie up in familiar embraces. And they weren't moving to Philadelphia either, where things were so different. She hid under Grandma's vanity and watched the sun bars moving across the polished wood floor.

3

The ring of the telephone reached out a long finger and poked Jeanie under the chin. She raised her head, listened, then hauled herself off the bed. The memory held her mind like a web from which she couldn't untangle, even after she heard Gail Macellaney's excited voice over the wire.

"Hi, it's me. Can you hold on a second?"

The relief of being home from work, nesting in her own apartment, washed over her body. Her back still hurt a bit at the waist from bending forward over the cash register. She glanced out the kitchen window where the last streak of sunlight faded on a brick wall. Except for the window in the living room, which looked out on a tall, bare tree, all her windows faced brick walls. The renting agent had told her if she waited a month she might have a sunnier apartment, but Jeanie had grabbed this one. It was like a cave buried in the city, remote from traffic, the perfect hideaway.

She could hear Gail helping husband Jake find his car keys. Gail, she thought, was lucky to be a first generation leftist, protester, revolutionist. She had the sparkle of new silver, while Jeanie's faith was pitted and tarnished by generations of waiting. Yet after she left the Church of All, Jeanie clung to Gail Macellaney, hoping to reflect some of her shine.

"Okay. I'm back. Tell me."

"Where were the car keys?"

"In his pocket, where else? Did you do it? Did you call him?"

"Yeah."

"Well, what did he say?"

"I didn't talk to him."

"Ohhhh."

Gail had been urging her to call Market for months. She felt Jeanie would not rest until she'd tried to pull something out of the ashes of her past. Sometimes she seemed more enthusiastic about the exposé than Jeanie herself.

"I spoke to his assistant, Gail. He was very interested. He said Market would definitely call me tonight."

"So it's on?"

"Yes, it started hours ago." Jeanie leaned against the refrigerator bouncing the long telephone cord. "Gail, I need you to take care of Lee tomorrow."

"What—pick her up from school?"

"I'm not sending her to school. Brainstorm showed up at her school today."

There was a silence and Jeanie could almost hear Gail clattering to conclusions. "So they know."

"I'd like to drop Lee off early. Is that okay?"

"Yes, of course, but what about tonight? Do you want to come over here? Oh no, you have to wait for the phone call. Do you want me to come over there?"

"No. Paul is coming later." She looked up at the kitchen

clock. "In fact he should have been here a long time ago. I hope he hasn't forgotten."

"You're not so easy to forget."

Jeanie peered at the clock as if it could tell her something more than the time. Paul was not usually late. "I hope he shows," she said. "I really should have told him before. Now it's going to seem like such a dramatic big deal."

"Last week you said you were going to let him in on it gradually."

"I showed him Eli Zinger's painting one night. But he didn't seem to catch the significance of it, and we got to talking about other things. It's really like a vacation being with Paul."

"So when do you think you'll see Eddie Market?"

"Tomorrow, I hope. Now that Brainstorm's located me I want to get it over with fast. Can you call in sick for me tomorrow?"

"Sure. But if you end up on TV . . ."

"Look, that manager must fall asleep right after supper. I can't imagine him staying up for the Eddie Market show."

Gail laughed and Jeanie wished she could be near her friend to see her rapidly peaking eyebrows and the yearning forward of her body, instead of the instrument hanging on her kitchen wall.

"I'm not feeling very good about all this," Jeanie admitted.

"What's the matter?"

"Oh, I don't mind giving him the information I have. But if he starts to ask all sorts of personal questions . . ."

"Yeah, that'd be rough," Gail said. "But you can surely handle it now. The more honest you are the more you can help other people."

"Oh, I just don't believe that," Jeanie said. "When Brainstorm and I decided to go off with Eli Zinger nothing that was said on television could have dissuaded us. Nothing. I'm afraid Market will ask about my background, and how I'm living now. . . ."

"I think you can set the limits. Tell him from the beginning what you want to tell and what you want to keep private."

Jeanie stared at the kitchen clock again, wondering why Paul was not there. He was never late before. He wouldn't be late. He was probably not coming. He must have decided there were no empty spaces in her life for him. Lee and Jeanie and her lockerful of secrets. She couldn't handle any extra complications. He was probably like all the other men who'd revolved through her bedroom door this year. What ever made her think he was different? He got the point about Eli Zinger's painting and decided to find himself a nice Italian girl who hasn't been around. Why should he come here when he can go back to his mother's brick house with red roses growing up a white trellis?

"Gail, I'm sure Paul isn't coming. I just know it."

"Don't be so jumpy."

"This guy Paul was never right for me in the first place. We're miles apart ideologically. I mean, trying to explain my background to him would be like . . . like trying to teach Leelannee sword swallowing."

Gail's laugh was too high-pitched over the phone. "You're upset because of Brainstorm. Paul will be there. If he doesn't come in an hour, call me back. Now, I'm supposed to fill you in on the coalition meeting we had today."

"Did they say anything about me?"

"Jeanie. They only asked why you weren't there. We talked about how to build on the momentum once the Church of All is exposed."

"Who says there's going to be a momentum?"

"Look, remember in the antiwar movement we used to build—"

"Them days are gone forever," Jeanie said, thinking that she sounded just like Aunt Claire.

"We're in a new period now, it's true, but we still have to remember that after a big news event people are left with a lot of unanswered questions and that's a good time to organize."

"Okay, don't give me the old rat-a-tat-a-tat right now, Gail. Paul is late. The address of Leelannee's school is no longer a secret." She almost added about the green Chrysler, but stopped herself. "Did anything happen at the meeting?"

"Yeah. Dave Yarrow from the taxi union split. He said he was sure his union would walk if they don't do something about this crisis, so he doesn't need a radical coalition, he can do it all through his union. We tried to talk to him about how he needed outside support, but he had his mind made up. He took all the drivers out with him."

Gail spoke as if Yodel represented tens of thousands of taxi drivers, but Jeanie knew he was the leader of only the tiny radical caucus. It was significant or insignificant depending on how involved you were personally.

"So what do you think about Yarrow?" Gail asked.

"I don't know. I'm not thinking about anything but how I'm gonna get through the next few days. I gotta get off. Maybe Paul is trying to call." She held the phone with her shoulder and began to wash the dishes in the sink. The water warmed her fingers and she rinsed the dishes longer than she had to. She cleaned the cereal pot with satisfaction. Nothing gave her as much a sense of competent motherhood as sending the child off to school with a hot breakfast. But there were innumerable days, after late meetings or nights of self-doubt, when she was lucky if the child had time to eat anything in the morning.

"I'm sorry to see the taxi drivers go," Gail said. "But they'll be back. If not for this crisis, then for the next."

"The next?"

"Well, sure. There's certainly gonna be more crises. This isn't the first one the system has thrown on us and it won't be the last. It's inevitable."

Jeanie laughed. "Oh, inevitable. I ate inevitable everyday for lunch when I was a kid."

"Shut up, you shit," Gail laughed. "It's very misleading to look at things in isolation. You have to look for the connections, the relationships. What you're doing with Eddie Market is just one aspect. . . ."

"Gail, I'm real jumpy. I'll see you tomorrow, okay? Early."

"Look, Jeanie, when you talk to Market don't forget to bring up this business with the crisis and how it connects with the Church of All bringing their urban crusade to town at this particular time."

"I won't forget. I'll see you tomorrow." Jeanie hung up smiling. Gail Macellaney always left her plated with a thin coat of optimism. She walked around the living room picking up stray newspapers and sweaters, feeling Gail in the rat-a-tat rhythm of her brain. Pick-it-up, pick-it up, stuff-it-in-the-drawer. The benign beat of her friend drew her to abstract thoughts. Inevitable, indeed. Oh, in the ultimate sense Jeanie guessed a revolution was inevitable. The human race would not survive unless it improved its social organization. But inevitable, when, in whose lifetime, and, even more important, would the inevitable change bring all the joy they thought it would? Or would it be, like a glow of the first All commune, only the superficial shine of newness?

She commanded herself to stop brooding about the inscrutable. A note from Faye lay on her bookshelf. A green Chrysler had followed her from the station. And Paul was late. She woke Leelannee gently, washed the child's face, and asked her to pick up her toys before she turned on the TV. How dare Paul be late? Didn't he know she panicked easily? She returned to the bathroom to wash her face, staring at her dripping skin in the mirror. She was a bit much for any man. "Something to contend with," as her father used to say. Brainstorm could never take her on her own terms. He never liked her to comment on his driving, or even to ask where they were going. But how terrible if Paul had really deserted her. He liked her dripping wet; he liked her in the morning with nothing but thirty years on her face; he laughed and slowed down the car when she told him he was driving too fast. She scrubbed at her skin and opened her eyes into handfuls of cool water. Then she dried on a cream-colored towel and patted her face with freshener. It was possible that he had a good reason. Car breakdown. Traffic jam. A call from his ex-wife. A cardiac arrest. She could always hope it wasn't a case of simple abandonment.

She brushed her hair vigorously until the static floated strands of electric red and brown above her head. Eerie. She smiled at her reflection. Eerie and clean. I might as well start dinner. Even if he doesn't come Leelannee has to eat. I'm hungry. She walked toward the kitchen collecting bits of lint from the rug.

4

Paul Moscato pulled up alongside a dark-green Chrysler. "Going out?" he asked the man who was sitting in the car with the inside light on. The man shook his bald head, not looking up from the needlepoint canvas on his lap. He was working on the trembly legs of a baby deer standing for the first time.

Paul found a spot that was almost big enough for his 1969 Chevrolet convertible about three blocks from Jeanie's house. He backed into the spot, touching bumpers with the car behind him and pushing it back until its tires rocked against the curb. Then he pushed the small car in front of him out of the way and parked. The spring warmth had disappeared with the sun and a strong wind was picking up. Fifty miles an hour, the radio predicted for tonight. Paul whistled along the darkened streets.

Dinner was ready to put on the table when the bell rang. Leelannee ran down the long hallway, struggling with the locks, while Jeanie stood for a moment in the kitchen. Ah, so he came. False panic. I can trust my intuitions, except when it comes to lovers. With lovers I haven't got a clue. She pictured her intuition as a mangy dog running down the beach with one leg limp and dragging. Work/politics/kid: these are my strong legs. But men—I'm lame.

Paul was bent, talking to Leelannee. He still had his coat on. Kneeling, he compressed his body to a less threatening size. "What's the matter?" he poked Leelannee. "You're not talking to me any more? I thought you were my friend. I thought you were going to tell me all your secrets. All your mother's secrets."

"I'm not," Leelannee said.

He stood up and caught Jeanie in his arms. "God, I missed you. Don't send me away for so long again."

His face was cold from outside. She tried to free herself. Her cheek pressed hard against his stubble. The embrace felt too sudden, too familiar. He just walked in the door. Hang up his coat, give him a drink, ask him how his day went. He held on, lifting her chin, grinning into her eyes.

"I missed you too," she said.

"No, you didn't. I don't believe you."

"I did," she laughed, trying to wiggle out of his arms, "I had a meeting last night. . . ."

"Meetings. Dates. Assignations. Secret assignments. Do you work for a foreign government?"

Leelannee pulled on Jeanie's sweater and she reached down a hand to stroke the child's hair.

"Don't be silly. Let me go, Paul. I have to check the meat."

"I can't let go. I'm stuck. I have to ask you something." They stumbled against the wall.

"You just got here, Paul."

"I might forget. And it's very important."

"What?"

"If you say no I'll throw myself out the window."

"I have bars on the window. Paul, let go of me!" She tickled him and he released her, following her to the kitchen as she ran to stir the beef stroganoff.

"Jeanie, don't do this to me again. I want to sleep with you every night. Do you hear? Every night."

Jeanie caught Leelannee's eye as the child sidled against the doorway. "Take your coat off, Paul."

"I want your answer by midnight," he said, unzippering his blue storm coat and walking down the hall to hang it up.

Leelannee pulled on Jeanie's sweater. "Bend down."

Jeanie checked the rice and tried to remember what she had left to do for the dinner. Her mind was full of him. She thought it was almost better to think about being with Paul than to actually be with him. At this first awkward stage of their relationship his presence made her so nervous that she had trouble remembering who she was.

He was soon back, filling up the archway with his large body, acting like he was in love. When the business with

Eddie Market was over maybe she'd have time to figure out if she was in love.

"Ma! Bend down. I want to ask you something."

Jeanie bent for the secret. "Mommy. What I want to know is this. Mommy!"

"Yeah. Go ahead, Lee. Hurry up."

"Mommy." She held on to Jeanie's neck. "Are you going to marry Paul?"

Paul heard the loud whisper and smiled at Jeanie, waiting for the answer.

"Well," she stirred the gravy around with her wooden paddle, "first he has to pass the tests, then I'll decide."

"What tests, Mommy?"

"Oh, you know, Leelannee. He has to spin straw into gold and come sailing over the Bronx in a ship that moves on land, water, and air."

Jeanie slid the hot plates of food on the table with the manner of an impertinent waitress, she thought, rather than a loving homemaker. Don't let him get any wrong ideas. "Go wash your hands, Leelannee."

Paul sat heavily in his chair and Jeanie thought she saw a crust of exhaustion under the grin. "How you been doing?"

"Worrying about you. Missing you. What'd you do to day? How was work?"

Jeanie shredded the meat on Leelannee's plate. "Work was all right. Not too much harassment. I think the assistant manager was too stoned to notice anything. I took a nice long coffee break—made a few phone calls." She thought she could just slip the story in right here, naturally, but there was too much going on with eating and Leelannee. It could wait. "Did you ever notice the waterfall you can see from the IRT after 174th Street?"

Paul shook his head. "Why? Did they turn it off today?"

"No," she laughed. "It's just that when I want to give

myself a treat I stand up and get a look at it from the train. I did that today."

"You're really a country girl."

Her face twisted. "I've seen my share of the country. I did my time in the woods. I want there to be beautiful things in the city."

"Run for mayor," he said. "I'll vote for you."

She looked at him blankly. He was trying to get her attention but she was thinking about whether Eddie Market had been the right newsman to call, and if he'd call back, and if the green Chrysler was still on Lydig Avenue. She wanted Paul with her, but in the back seat, not at the steering wheel. The strain of resisting the natural flow of conversation was giving her a headache.

She stared at Leelannee's plate until the child reluctantly picked up her fork. It was a pleasure to cook for Paul. Never any leftovers.

Paul's glance traveled from mother to daughter. "Sometimes in this apartment I feel like an anthropologist visiting a cave-dwelling tribe that never uses language except for ceremonial occasions. You and Lee communicate by looks and breathing."

Jeanie worried about how she would begin to tell him. The first sentence would be the hardest. If only I'd told him little by little, hint by hint from the beginning. People from my background learn to keep secrets. And who knew he'd still be revolving through my door? Who knew he'd want to bring his suitcase? "Why don't you turn on the TV?" she said. "Time for the news."

"I hate the news," he said. "Emergency! Emergency! Disco fire kills forty-two. Earthquake swallows a village in Peru. Plane drops hundred and six in the Atlantic."

"Turn it on," she laughed. "Tonight they may be playing my disaster."

He reached over and pulled out the knob. They watched a car being displayed from all sides. "And by the time I get it," Paul said, "it'll be on its third set of tires with dents in the doors and a big hole in the tailpipe."

Jeanie shushed him as the crisis story came on. Going to coalition meetings had made it her crisis, and she listened to the latest pronouncements by leading cabinet members and officials with total interest, though Paul never stopped talking.

"So we got a crisis of confidence, a crisis of currency, a crisis in petroleum. Next they're going to tell you there's a hospital, fire, police, welfare, and garbage strike coming off at midnight. . . ."

"Shhhh," Jeanie laughed, filling Lee's fork and staring at the TV.

"I can't get excited over this stuff. I just can't get involved."

"If you're not involved you might as well be dead," Jeanie said. Boy, wouldn't that be easy, just to not watch the news, not view yourself as an active participant bound to choose up sides on every question. It was not one of her options. History was hoisted onto her shoulders at an early age. It was unthinkable to abandon the future.

The crisis story was over and the commentator previewed the next item: "We'll be right back with the story of the guru and the Senator's daughter." The screen flashed Eli Zinger's bearded face, which was open with laughter. Then it switched to an airline commercial showing people sawing away at their dinner with plastic knives.

"Did you see that guy?" Jeanie asked Paul. She regretted having caused the uncomfortable look on his face; when she was a kid her father always watched the news during dinner and she always resented it.

"Which one?" Paul said.

"The guy with the beard."

"Oh, your friend the painter." Paul cleared the dishes

from the table, stacking plates on top of forks. "I wanted to ask you—is he for real or some kind of an actor?"

Jeanie thought a moment, staring at the commercial and pulling on her hair. "He's sincere in his way. He doesn't have any self-doubt. If he thinks something, or says something, then he's sure it's true because, after all, he said it."

"One more time," Paul said.

"He thinks he's infallible. Maybe when he was a kid his mother told him he was perfect all the time and he just believed her. Hey Leelannee, you know what?"

"What? I don't want any more meat."

"You're not perfect, Leelannee. Pretty close, but not quite perfect."

The commercial dissolved into a sea of young New Yorkers smiling up at the TV camera with goodness glowing on their cheeks. On the second-floor balcony of the Reverence Hotel Eli Zinger—bearded, smiling, very relaxed despite the wind that whipped his hair—was speaking to the crowd. Next to him, the announcer said, was Senator Carpenter's daughter Helena, a tiny, birdlike girl whose head was cocked toward Eli Zinger.

"The Senator must be having a fit," Paul said.

"I'm not so sure."

After a few gravely sounds the microphone picked up Zinger's speech. "Capitalism is in ruins. Socialism is in ruins. Fascism stalks like a resurrected beast on its last hungry prowl. The soul of the world vibrates in true protest against the sins of state. What we all need is peace, and peace will be given to those who reach for it. We can transcend together with a sigh, like pollen on the winds of change. We can transcend together." The camera zoomed in on Zinger's impassioned face, as he listened to the surge of chanting from the crowd.

"What are they saying?" Paul asked.

"I think it's 'Your wish is my command.' His voice is

even better in person. It sounds like smoke and fire. You can't help listening to him."

The image switched to a newsman at the studio desk. "After the rally, Allees scattered through the downtown area selling ten-dollar tickets for tomorrow night's midnight mass at Manhattan Garden."

Jeanie snapped off the TV as a story about a fire in Queens came on. Eli Zinger's speech had sounded freshly compelling. Like a moon in eclipse, his voice pulled tidal waves of feelings in her. Nostalgia for the girl she once was. Regret for all those years. "He sure manages to get free commercials," she said to Paul.

"How'd you meet him?"

"It was my great misfortune." She tried to ride out the wave without toppling. "That was in my hippie days, you see."

Paul tilted back his chair. "I didn't know you had hippie days. What days are these?"

"These are my working-class days." She punched an imaginary cash register and pulled groceries toward her.

"Uh huh. And after this?"

She shook her hair out of her eyes. "I'm open for suggestions." That was the wrong thing to say. She wanted to snatch back the words.

"How well do you know Zinger?" Paul asked.

Jeanie sat down in the living room, waiting for him to follow. It was starting and she didn't have to worry about first sentences. She just hoped it wouldn't burn down what they had together. "I knew him very well for a while."

"While you were married, or before you were married, or after you split up?"

The questions confused her. What did it have to do with being married? "No," she said, "it was my job. My mission in life. I was his political officer."

The telephone rang but she just sat there listening to the rings. This was the last exit before the toll. She didn't have to pick it up. If she didn't pick it up perhaps the green Chrysler would vanish in the night.

"It's for you," Paul said finally.

She stood leaning against the refrigerator as she waited for Eddie Market's secretary to put him on the line. It was after seven—she wondered if the secretary was getting paid overtime.

"This is Eddie Market," he said in the flawless, mellow voice that went so well with the shirtsleeve look on television. "Am I speaking to Ms. Burger?"

"Yes."

"Ms. Burger, you called me concerning the Church of All, didn't you?"

"Yes."

"I was just watching their rally now on the news. Did you happen to catch it?"

"Yes, we were just watching," Jeanie said, letting him lead, surprised that it was so easy.

"What was your impression? Do you think they'll score a big success in New York?"

"Well, I hope not. I find them very scary. With this crisis of confidence we have now it's a great time for Zinger to step in and pick up the strays. I know something about how he manages to do that, and . . . and some documents you might like to take a look at."

"Yes, Bob said you mentioned that."

"He's the assistant?"

"Yes."

"Who else knows that I called you?" She hoped she wasn't stepping on her credibility. If she sounded paranoid he might just hang up. "The reason I ask," she said, eyeing Paul, who was openly listening, "is that my ex-husband is still with All. And somehow he found out where I am today."

"Have you been underground?" Market asked. It was obvious he enjoyed saying the word, as if it had magical significance.

"No—not exactly."

"I guess several people in my office might have seen your message," Market admitted. "If you think you're in danger we should get the police in on this."

How dangerous are they? Despite all the information she had, she couldn't imagine them as truly dangerous. She had been part of it once. Now there were forces she didn't like in control, but surely Eli Zinger was not of criminal mentality.

"It's okay," she told Market. "I'd just like to see you kind of quickly."

"How's tonight for you?"

"No, not tonight." Not that quickly. She needed a chance to reassemble, to explain to Paul. "How about tomorrow, early?"

"Fine. In my office?"

"Yes."

"Will you be coming alone?"

She wondered at the question, gazing at Paul's powerful shoulders. "No. I'm gonna bring my bodyguard."

"Fine," Market laughed. "Give me his name so I can leave it with the security desk. They're very strict around here."

Leelannee was dozing on Paul's lap. He looked at Jeanie, his purple-brown eyes full of brooding questions. She tried to brake her screeching thoughts. With a trembling arm she led Leelannee off to bed and sat in the dark with the child, patting her bottom. She sat there long after Leelannee had fallen asleep, chewing her tongue, reluctant to go back to Paul and explain. Whatever she said would be starting in the middle. She couldn't explain why she'd left All, without telling why she'd joined to begin with. None of it would make any sense unless she explained her background, and that wasn't something you casually undraped for a lover of five weeks who'd probably never met anyone from a communist home before. The tidal wave of feelings Eli Zinger had released in her began to subside. She stopped hearing Market's confident voice. She landed back on herself, wet, cold, anxious to wrap herself in a familiar blanket. The comfort came to her in pieces, in fragments. The way she'd taken on causes as if she was choosing freely. The way she'd learned who she was aside from Mother's child, molding herself to be worthy of her heritage, becoming someone to contend with.

Attendance. "Here."

"Absent." Hah hah. Someone always said "absent."

"Jeanette." Miss Maguire's voice was like a knife.

"Here."

"Pencil? Hold it up."

"Here."

"Handkerchief? Dog tag? Where's your dog tag, Jeanette?"

She slid down on the flat wooden seat. She stuck her hand in her desk, pretending to look.

"I'm speaking to you, Jeanette."

"My mother wrote a note. I gave it to you yesterday."

"Would you please speak up."

"The note from my mother. I gave it to you."

"Humph! Yes. I remember."

Jeanie wondered if communists really called themselves communists or was that a bad word like nigger that other people called them? Mother said she would write a note saying Jeanie couldn't be in the air raid drills too. Maybe she'll forget. Jeanie decided not to tell her when the class crouched on the floor, crawled under the slanting wooden desks, and wrapped their arms around their heads. It was the most exciting part of school. She was always waiting for it. She wanted to sleep down there on the cool floor with her arms wrapped around her ears. She could almost hear the airplanes coming.

"Jeanie, the teacher says you're not learning. When the other children work you're looking out the window."

Sometimes there were snowflakes out the window. And she had to keep her eye out for the airplanes. Her father was looking at her, very sad and serious. "There's no school tomorrow," she said.

"Oh, Lincoln's birthday, huh?" He draped his newspaper over the arm of his chair. "Did the teacher tell you anything about Lincoln?"

"She said about slaves. What's a slave? Lincoln freed the slaves and tomorrow there's no school."

He rubbed his chin where the red stubble went scratch scratch. "Slaves were workers who didn't get paid. People with black skin, like Marcus from the next building, were slaves."

"Marcus is a slave? Really? A real slave?"

"No. His grandmother was a slave, maybe, when she was a little girl. A long time ago. Evelyn, were Marcus's people from the North or the South?"

Evan ran through with his gun belt on over his pajamas. She slid off her father's lap.

"Wait, Jeanie. Did you know that slaves weren't allowed to read or write?"

"They didn't have to go to school?"

"They weren't *allowed* to go. If the master caught them reading a book they could be killed."

"*Killed*? Killed dead?"

Evan took out both cap shooters and pretended to shoot. Kew! Kew! He wasn't allowed to shoot caps in the house.

Daddy held out an arm and she climbed back in his lap. "How come the slaves couldn't be allowed to read?"

"Because, Jeanie, if people read books they learn about things. They get ideas. They learn that other people are not slaves. Other workers get paid for their work. They want to be free. A lot of slaves learned to read anyway."

"Weren't they afraid of being *killed*?"

"Yeah, I guess so, but they did it anyway. They wanted to be free."

It started to lick at her heart, hotter and hotter, until she burned to read, to get ideas, to be free. February, March, April, May. In May Miss Maguire put a dumb star on her workbook. The brick houses across the street from the school all had red roses climbing up white Y-shaped trellises. The most beautiful red roses on green oily leaves. Once a lady let her take a rose that lay on the grass, but when she picked it up all the petals fell out. If you lived in the projects you didn't have roses growing in the yard. But she was always glad to get home from the thick smell of roses. Something was always happening at home.

The day the spring rain was falling Father said he was taking Evan for a haircut. Onfredo from next door and Marcus from the next building were going too. It wasn't fair. Every other time Jeanie had to take Evan for his stupid haircut by herself. On the wall of the barber shop there was a picture of a tall blond girl in a cowboy vest with nothing but big breasts underneath, and a short fringed skirt that left a long stretch of leg exposed down to the boot. Jeanie wanted to see what happened when her father saw that calendar. He would rip it right off the wall. She begged to go along with them to the barber shop but he said no until her mother said, "Oh, take her, Jay."

The group of them walked very slowly and kept stopping to talk. They stopped right under the elevator train with the rain dripping through the tracks. They didn't remember to hold Jeanie's hand when they crossed the street.

They sat in a row on the leather bench. The men getting haircuts looked at them through the mirror. Jeanie didn't like them watching her. Father talked quietly to Marcus and he didn't look at the cowgirl calendar. Jeanie didn't look at it either.

When the boss in the first chair finished brushing the hair off his customer he walked over to them. "Marcus here is next," Father said.

The barber shook his head slowly. "I don't know how to cut that kind of hair."

Jeanie looked at Marcus's hair. He had the kind of black hair that curled like the wire on a spiral notebook. His skin was dark, with a shine on it. He was tall and muscled like a man ready to leap a fence.

"Let me introduce myself. I'm Marcus Walker. This is Jay Burger and Onfredo Antonioni." They all shook hands.

"We come from the Tenant's League, from the projects," Onfredo said, "to speak to you about this."

"You know my kids can't get a haircut in this neighborhood," Marcus said. "Me—I can get one in a Negro barbershop near where I work. But my kids—where are they supposed to go?"

The barber kept wiping his hands on his white shirt. "I'm sorry for you, Mr. Walker, but I just don't know how to cut that kind of hair. Never did it in my life. Look, if it was just up to me, I don't mind at all. But my customers—they wouldn't like it. I got my business to think about."

Father had his hand on the barber's shoulder. "I know you're a decent guy. You don't believe in Jim Crow."

The barber shook his head. "Don't believe in it at all—but my customers."

"You know Cappacini's shop, on the other side of the projects?" Father asked.

"Of course I know Cappacini." He looked up from his shoes.

"Well, some other people from the Tenant's League are going over there today about this. And we decided to throw up a picket line if the owners don't . . . have the courage to stand up for what they believe in."

"A picket line? This is a union shop!" His voice was like the scrape of a razor along the sharpening strap. Jeanie felt scared and ran next to her father. Evan held on to her hand.

Father drew back a step and Onfredo began to speak. "You know the Tenant's League is pretty strong at the projects."

Jeanie was surprised to hear the way they kept mentioning they lived at the projects as if it was a great place to live, as if it wasn't a whole lot worse than those little brick houses with roses growing in the yard.

"We've got a bunch of these Negro families who are having a problem about haircuts," Onfredo said. "It's ridiculous for them to take their kids to Harlem for a haircut. This is their neighborhood too."

"A picket line? Just what I need—a picket line. You think it's easy for a small business these days?"

Marcus walked slowly to the first chair and sat down. The owner trundled after him. "A picket line! I already signed with the union. How do you want me to cut your hair, Mr. Walker from the Tenant's League?"

As Marcus was showing him, Father and Onfredo and Evan sat down in the other chairs and the barbers began to cut their hair. Jeanie sat back on the leather bench alone, breathing deeply, sparkling with what she had witnessed. They would talk about this over and over at home, she knew. It was important; you *could* change things; that's why you didn't wear a dog tag to school even if it was against regulations, even if it made you squirm and feel funny, it was worth it because you *could* change things. She was startled out of her thoughts by Onfredo.

"What do you think of her, Jay?" he said, pointing to the big-vested cowgirl calendar. "You like them that tall?"

Father looked right at the picture. Jeanie thought it might go up in flames or fall off its thumbtack. She was suffocating from swallowing her breath.

"I don't know," Father shrugged. "You'll have to ask my wife, she's the boss of the family."

Jeanie breathed out and almost slid off the leather bench. Nothing else happened. He had looked straight at the girl in the cowboy vest with nothing but big breasts underneath and a long stretch of leg from her fringed skirt to her boot and nothing happened. He didn't knock it off the wall. The building did not smolder and burn. She tried to suck in all the things that did not happen, slumping down a little more in the oily, sweet-smelling barber shop. Her father had to shake her to get her up when it was time to leave. The men all looked funny with their new haircuts making their ears stand out.

"Let's head over to Cappacini's shop," Marcus said, "and see how the others made out."

"I'm going to go to Sally's," Jeanie told her father. She didn't want to hear them bragging about everything. She wanted to be with Sally, who had seen the calendar too, who wore pink glasses and spoke in gulping whispers about her five older brothers and the manhole system they used to escape from rival gangs. Sally knew things. She knew about the numbers written on the telephone booth wall, and the slouchy neighborhood cop who didn't pay for his lunch at the Sweet Shoppe.

Sally was home alone. She had her own key. When the rain finally stopped the girls walked around the neighborhood and ended up, as they always did, next to the storefront coat factory where Sally's mother worked. They hung around the door, which was propped open to let the air reach the row of women working at a long table. Jeanie read the ILGWU union card in the window. She knew about unions. The big sewing machines buzzed on and off under the eye of the short owner with a dead cigar in his mouth.

The girls edged into the shop sideways. Overhead on the rack, cut pieces of navy blue cloth were being pushed along: one woman sewing the seams together, the next sewing sleeves, the next tacking in the lining, then buttonholes, collars. Sally's mother worked at the far end of the store finishing the seams. She smiled at them, then tossed a wrinkled forehead toward the boss, who stood like a school monitor looking out the yellowed window. She put coins in their hands.

"Go. Get some ice cream. Don't get ices, only ice cream, hear? Go out and play, Sally. Get some air. Where are your brothers?"

Sally never answered a question. She leaned her face against her mother's shoulder. "Tell your brothers to take care of you. Go—go out and play in the air."

They walked as slowly as they could, dragging their shoes through the scraps of blue wool on the floor. Jeanie watched the fingers feeding material into the machines. She heard them talking and laughing over the uneven whirrs of the wheels. There was Angelina who was so beautiful a man could fall dead looking at her. That's what the heavy woman said. The heavy woman, with bits of cotton fuzz stuck to the sweat on her forehead, put her arm around Jeanie. The wet spreads under her arms reached almost to her waist. "Isn't our Angelina beautiful? I'm waiting for the days she comes in here with a diamond ring on her finger. . . ."

"I'm beautiful?" Angelina laughed, shaking her head. "Look at the child you're talking to. She's beautiful—out in the sun all the time."

Jeanie thought they were all beautiful, even the fat old ones. She loved to watch their fingers feed cloth into the machines. Stop, start. The heavy woman took a picture out of her wallet: her children, her husband, herself all dressed up for something. The monitor at the dirty window took the dead cigar out of his mouth and sighed so loud they could hear it over the sewing machines.

"Come on," Sally said, "you'll get my mother in trouble."

Jeanie felt better as she walked from the shop. Watching them work, watching them turn the big navy triangles into smart winter coats with brass buttons, it didn't seem so bad to be a girl, to be a woman some day with breasts sticking out of her body. To have her picture in some man's wallet, not stuck on a calendar in a barber shop.

But it didn't all come together until some school day in the week after that. "You're the only *girl* who gets into trouble," Miss Maguire said, but it didn't scare Jeanie. She knew who she was. She was the kid with red hair from the projects who wrote on her desk and knew that it was possible to change things. What did Marble-Eyed Maguire know? She put her hand right over her breast when she said the Pledge of Allegiance. Didn't she see the boys laughing? She wiped tears from the corners of her glass-blue eyes when they sang "God Bless America." Didn't she know the truth about God? About America?

5

Paul was unbuttoning his blue workshirt when Jeanie returned to the living room. Her eyes adjusted slowly to the bright light. She smiled at him, glad he was so easy to look at, feeling beautiful herself under his warm gaze. She hugged his waist, helping to pull the shirt off his shoulders. "Come on, I thought you'd be all undressed by now." Then she found herself facing a gold Hines beer label on Paul's undershirt. "Well, what have we here? Another human billboard?"

Paul looked around as if he didn't know who she was talking to.

"I think it's wonderful for you to offer your body to a beer company for advertising purposes. You know, all day long at Mirrormart I check out counterfuls of name brand this and that, and there are the people posing as groceries too. Hats with beer cans on them, shirts with gas company emblems, tote bags with classy perfume de urgency. . . . And when we die we'll have 'plant a greener lawn' stickers on our coffins."

Paul pulled off his T-shirt and wadded it in his hand. "How can you be sarcastic about my favorite undershirt?"

"No, I think its very touching that you want to wear the brand of your oppressor. I bet you paid three ninety-eight for the honor of giving free advertising to that corporation."

"I paid a dollar on Fourteenth Street. I happen to like Hines beer. But," he tossed the shirt into a wastebasket and held her face in the soft brown hair on his chest, "I surrender to your political analysis. After all, you were political officer for Eli Zinger, so you must know what you're talking about."

He didn't let her pull away, but stroked her hair until

she relaxed against him. "My political education did *not* begin with Eli Zinger."

"You know, I told my mother all about you yesterday. I was raving from not seeing you. My mother asked me how I met you." Jeanie raised her eyes to his. "I said, Ma, remember when some of the guys dragged me down to that demonstration? Yeah, you told me not to go, Ma, but it turned out to be a very lucky day."

Jeanie squirmed in his arms, trying to step back to gauge his seriousness, but he didn't let her go.

"Be still, that's a good girl. Don't interrupt me when I'm talking to my mother. So I said, well, Ma, do you remember the spot on TV about some supermarket checkers who threw rocks at the mayor's office? There she was, Ma . . . no, not on TV, live, in person, and she had the best aim—her rock really hit the window, Ma."

"You didn't really say that."

"So my mother says, 'Just what we need, another hothead in the family. It's not enough that your cousin Mario gambles.' "

Jeanie threw her weight forward and toppled him over on the bed, falling on top of him. He twisted a strand of her hair around his finger. "I love the way your hair curls one way on this side and the other way on the other side."

"Paul," she sighed. "We have to talk."

"You know what I really want to know?"

"What?"

"Are you seeing anyone else?"

"Seeing?"

"Dating. I mean were you with some guy last night."

She laughed, shaking her head, no, no, no. "I hardly have time for you."

He scratched her head, scratched the back of her neck, flopped her over on the bed and gave her a very brisk, unmethodical back rub. "My toy," he laughed. Then he pushed her head into the pillow and covered her with the spread. "Okay, let's sleep. I had a very rough day today."

"Did you? You seem in such a good mood."

"Lock the triple bolt on your door. Set the alarm clock. Shut the lights. Put the milk away. This is your house, you know."

She sat up. "You can't go to sleep yet. We've got so many things to talk about."

"Tomorrow," he said, turning on his stomach.

"Paul. It's only nine o'clock. I can make some coffee."

"I never get enough sleep," he mumbled. "All my life I've been looking for an extra hour's sleep."

"Forget about sleeping. Look, do you have any plans for tomorrow?"

"I plan to sleep."

She prodded his ribs. "I'm going to need your help tomorrow."

"Fine. Whatever you want." He cocked his head. "What do they say—your wish is my command."

She shuddered. She didn't like hearing him allude to All, she didn't like thinking about it in his presence. It was terrible to give up the freshness of their relationship and let the past seep in. "I really do need your help tomorrow, Paul. And it might be dangerous."

"As long as it's not the laundry," he said, but he rolled over. "What do you mean dangerous?"

Well, what did she mean? Please please please. It was the vaguest of threats, only that it was delivered through the child. That was terrifying. And the green Chrysler . . . but maybe that was gone by now.

"Thinking," he knocked against her forehead. "I'm not paying you to think."

"What?"

"That's what my boss told me today. 'Moscato, I'm not paying you to think. See that the barge is lowered and unloaded by the time I get back.' Then he got in his Buick and drove away."

"What were you not supposed to think about?" They both sat up and folded pillows behind their backs.

"I don't want to think about it," he said. He looked worn and depressed under the gauze of his smile.

"Why don't you just tell me fast, so I'll know," she said.

"I don't know if you'll understand. Someday I'll have to take you out to City Island with me and show you where I work." His chest was rising and falling like the wind outside. "The barge is on these huge legs—this big around." He extended his arms in a fat circle. "The legs weigh about four tons each, see. You can move the barge up and down to rest on the water when the tide goes in and out, but it's a pain in the ass to move it; it's a big operation. I told the boss we should wait a couple of hours until the tide came in to unload. Then we wouldn't have to lower the barge. But he says, 'Moscato, do it my way,' and he exits."

Paul shook his head, his voice running down with weariness. "I was in charge of the operation. I thought this guy Cogan knew what he was doing, but he didn't, or he made a mistake. Something. You see each leg has a wheel and they all have to be turned at the same time. All of a sudden the barge tilted and fifty tons of iron slid right into the water. We could've been killed. Easy. We had to spend the rest of the afternoon hauling that stuff out of the Sound with the crane. Such a waste of energy. The tide would've come in in three hours."

"Was anyone hurt?" Jeanie leaned on her hands, watching his face, which looked like an irrigated plain.

"No. We were lucky. We all managed to jump out of the way when the iron started to slide. We were so pissed off though, let me tell you, it took hours to haul that iron out of the water. That's why I was so late coming over here, not that you even noticed."

"I noticed," she said. "I was sure you weren't coming at all."

"But meanwhile you made a fantastic dinner."

"Well . . ." She smiled. "So you had a real harassed day. Is your boss always a blockhead, or was it just . . ."

"He's not a blockhead. He figured we'd get the thing unloaded in an hour and he could send us home early and save some money. Might have worked out just that way if it wasn't for Cogan."

"In a socialist society the people who do the job have a say in how it's done. That makes a lot of sense to me," Jeanie said.

"In what socialist society?"

"In the one my grandparents were always waiting for. Maybe in China today, from what I've heard."

He laid his hand heavily on her thigh. "I can't imagine it any different than it is."

"Can't you?" A feeling of ideological pain seized her. He was really so different from her. She couldn't look at any aspect of society without imagining it different than it was today. And there he was, resigned to what was.

Paul kicked her foot under the cover. "What? Why don't you tell me what you're thinking?"

She tried to get some words ready but there were no words, just a rush of feelings that wouldn't mix: the hot lava of anger, the oily distrust, the clear water of sympathy. He did have a hard day. He stared at her, his face rigid as a warrior on a Roman coin. Then he cracked into a smile. "You know what I like about you, Jeanie? You're so spontaneous. So open. Maybe you should just try and tell me about this dangerous laundry we have to do tomorrow."

Blurt it out, she commanded herself. Don't let the words congeal. She ticked off on her fingers. "First, we have to bring Lee over to my friend Gail's—do you remember Gail?"

"The one with the speeches?"

Jeanie laughed despite herself. "Right. Then we have to go downtown and pick up some papers. Then we have to bring them to Eddie Market at WEBD and see what he thinks. I don't know what's going to happen after that."

"Put making love on your list," he said, reaching under and squeezing her bottom.

"Ooo. I have a little free time right now." She leaned over and rubbed his stomach under his belt. Gail once told her that was a good trick, that men were sensitive where their clothes were tight.

"What kind of papers do you have that Eddie Market wants to see? Was that who you were talking to on the phone?"

She played more daringly. "Yes, that was him. The papers are about All. All I know about All. Enough to send them up the river for fifty years if we had a decent system of justice in this country."

She opened his pants buckle. It took her quite a while and he sat watching her, not helping. Then he pulled her back to his shoulder and stroked her cheeks. His hand was large and covered almost her whole face. They were too new together to undress quickly, so it took a time of tangled struggle until their clothes were off in lumps under the covers. He kissed her near the hairline. She had tangled her fingers in the black hair between his legs, but he moved a little out of her reach, still trying to talk.

"What did they do?"

"Who?"

"The Church of All."

"'Ohhh." She moved far away from him and leaned against the cold wall. "If you want to talk we can talk."

"But you don't want to?"

She pulled the cover up over her nose, peering over it. "Sure. Why not? What else have we got to do?" Then she dove under the cover, playing with him again. He knew enough for the time being. More than enough. She wanted to be assured that he was with her thus far, that he wasn't pulling back to figure out what he'd ever seen in her in the first place.

She was much more in a hurry than he was. He handled her breasts as if they were delicate and breakable. He kissed her shoulders, and her hands, giving her the reassurance she needed rather than the sex she expected. It was different from her experience. With Dennis there had been no play, just fuck fuck fuck to satisfaction—a gymnastic skill in which sex was uncluttered with personality. A naked vine. She was sorry to think of Dennis now, and Paul seemed to catch her inattention for he stopped arousing her and began to softly kiss her shoulders again.

She opened her eyes and tried to meet his purple gaze. His kind of sex seemed so ornate. The vine was covered with posies and thorns, sprouting odd buds of affection. She noticed how the age creases on his neck softened his skin. He acted as if he had years to spend in bed, but as her body began to ache from being touched so much he pulled her on top of him and let her knock herself out. He made whispering noises and called her darling. He squeezed her breasts sharply now that she was beyond feeling pain. She lifted his big hand to her cheek, imagining he was slapping her face again and again until she came. In a moment he had rolled her over and mounted a passion of his own. Her palms were alive and she ran them over the acres of skin of his full body. An image of the green Chrysler drifted through her mind. She wondered if Eddie Market had believed her. She held on to Paul tightly, smiling into the purple waters of his eyes, until he finished with her.

He heaved himself onto the pillow and fell asleep. She lay awake, thinking that she should have answered all his questions rather than cutting him off with kisses, but by the time she turned her sticky body over on her pillow she was asleep too.

6

Paul jumped when the bell shrilled. "Company?" He had pulled on his pants before Jeanie even stirred from the pillow. She moved slowly, zipping into a bathrobe, calling "just a minute" down the long corridor with its green daisy linoleum left by the former tenant. It was 10:30. Late for a neighbor to ring. She sniffed deeply to check for smoke. Then shook her head as Paul tucked in the bedspread. "No one would know you went to Catholic school."

Her damp thighs stuck together as she walked unsteadily down the hall. She pried open the peephole, looked at the wavery image, then dropped her hand and let it fall shut. The wave of heat that moved over Jeanie's body was so intense that she thought the metal door would not keep Faye from feeling it. How dare she come here? Perhaps she should just shout "not interested," as if Faye was some Jehovah's Witness ringing the bell early on Sunday morning. The bell shrilled again. Jeanie imagined Faye standing there, long into the night, ringing and ringing until Leelannee awoke and Paul grew angry. She would have to hear her out. Faye had no power here. This was Jeanie's apartment, her neighborhood, her life. Faye was just someone she used to know. Jeanie slowly unclicked the locks and opened the door.

Three gold discs blazed like badges from their chests. Three eager smiles. She should have guessed Faye would never go anywhere alone. "Eli sends greetings," Faye said merrily.

Jeanie kept the door half closed, leaning it on the foot the tall follower had put over the doorway. "What do you want?"

"Were you resting? Eli says you've been resting, Jeanette. But now it's time for us to touch spheres."

In the yellow light of the hallway Jeanie saw a deep crease stretched across Faye's forehead. She opened the door to let them in, moved that Faye no longer looked like a girl, that her silk robe was cut close to her body in desperation to adorn, unlike the casual flings of fabric Faye had worn in the past.

Faye entered the apartment, her arms stretched out toward Jeanie's shoulders. "It's so good to look at you again. If you're through resting, I would like to see this sight each day."

Jeanie thought of keeping the three intruders crowded in the corridor, away from Paul, but she finally led them forward to the light at the end of the hall.

Paul was leaning against the bookcase. Jeanie managed to shoot him a sign that she, too, was annoyed, before the members of the Church of All entered the room. She introduced Paul to Faye. "Thomas and Carla," Faye smiled at her escorts, directing them to sit on the couch. "Paul and Jeanette. Jeanette was one of the original inspirers," she explained. "You are seeing her in her worldly aspect, but if you can, imagine in her a most transcendant soul."

"Nice to meet you," Paul mumbled. "I didn't know Jeanie was expecting company."

Faye settled in a white wicker rocker, crossing her legs to the slither of silk. Dark eyes stared out above her perpetual smile. "We all live in a constant state of expectation," she said. "Thank God for that."

Paul's eyebrows shot up and he glanced at Jeanie, who experienced her past and present colliding with terrific speed. A constant state of expectation. She understood the words. They had once slid off her tongue like milk. She sat on the edge of the bed, which Paul had neatly made up. "Well," she found herself smiling almost as brightly as Faye.

"Well, I brought you a present." She tossed a velvet bag across the room and it landed heavily in Jeanie's lap. "Aren't you going to open it, your godship?"

Jeanie pulled the drawstrings of the small bag and took out a solid round of glass.

"Hold it against your eye," Faye said. "Have a new look at yourself. It's called iridology—a new science—an ancient one, too."

Jeanie looked at the three of them, smiling and poised in her apartment, their feet crossed on her black and white abstract rug, their eyes traveling over her boyfriend, her bedspread, her posters. It was hard to believe they were here. They were like apparitions, nodding in unison, their faces hooded with smiles. She raised the glass and saw a clear reflection of her own brown eyeball looming at her. She held it there as long as she dared, trying to think. They must be testing her seriousness, her strength. She had to get them out quickly, but politely, without incident. Finally she lowered the glass. "I'm not particularly interested in my own eyeball." If she could keep from returning Faye's smile, that alone would tell them something.

"There's a map of the eye, inside the bag. It explains what the pools and flecks of your iris reveal about your inner state. I can see from here that you are world-weary, Jeanette."

Jeanie shrugged, putting the glass back in the bag. "I don't know anything about this stuff any more. It's not what we talk about at work."

Faye wove her fingers together and leaned her chin on her hands. "That's no wonder. Eli explains that work will soon be obsolete. And it can't be too soon."

"That's the truth!" the girl on the couch chimed in.

Jeanie thought that if she pushed back, evenly, without sharp edges, they would begin to see. She turned to Paul. "For an organization that feels that work is obsolete, it's amazing how many people they've got working in factories producing All matches and decals and, probably, these eye mirrors."

Faye lifted her chin and eyebrows. "But you know that's not work. That's fundraising. It's entirely voluntary." She turned to the two on the couch, who nodded.

"Which means they don't get paid," Jeanie said. It was the debate she'd never had with Faye, with Eli Zinger, with Brainstorm, and she felt herself warming to it. She had left the commune suddenly, riding on her own sudden repulsion, but later she'd regretted leaving so much unsaid.

"You speak like an outsider Jeanette. Eli says you are only resting. When you get over Dennis you will return. We've come to collect you tonight."

Jeanie noted the stiff garnet and gold bracelet on Faye's wrist, the sparkling rings that glittered off her moving fingers. The appealing smile, like a child trying to delay her bedtime, seemed too innocent to go with jewels and silk. Carla, who was younger, seemed more natural in her joyousness. Thomas was something else altogether; too big for his smile, his body like an athlete who had gone to seed. They had come to collect her, had they? "Tell me, Faye, how's your father?"

Their eyes met and for a heartbeat of time Jeanie thought

now she will crack, the milky words will taste sour on her tongue, she will say what she feels. But Faye lifted herself out of the rocker in a long, graceful movement, still smiling. "Mr. Cordite is progressing well. Those who seek enlightenment after years of worldly contamination have special problems. Just as those who read too many books and fill their minds with contradiction and confusion." She motioned to Jeanie's overstuffed bookshelf, and the followers gazed in the direction of her hand.

"Books are forbidden in the Church of All," Jeanie explained to Paul, who looked as though he were listening to a foreign language and not anxious for a translation. "They had a mass book burning one day, not long before I left."

"We've begun our own press now," Faye said. "Jeanette, don't resist the attraction. Your soul is screaming for release. And Eli needs you so much just now. Come with us to see Eli this evening. He needs to talk to you as much as you to him."

"I have plans for the evening," Jeanie said.

In the silence that Jeanie let lengthen she could hear the scream of the wind rising and falling outside. Paul began to shift from one foot to the other. "Was it pretty bad when you drove up?" he asked the man on the couch.

Thomas nodded, his bald head gleaming.

"What kind of a car do you drive?"

Thomas glanced at Faye, who nodded. "A green Chrysler."

"Yeah, what year?"

Thomas stared at his fingers. "Cars are not of the essence," he said.

"That's the truth, Thomas," the girl next to him agreed, her cheeks turning pink.

Jeanie wondered why Faye had let her know that Thomas was the man in the Chrysler? He didn't look as thin or vegetarian as the other Allees, or as young; perhaps he shaved his head as a vanity against encroaching baldness. He rummaged in the pockets of his big overcoat, withdrew a needlepoint canvas, and began to stitch with a forward, rocking motion. The girl put her arm around his shoulders. There was something to that impersonal closeness, thought Jeanie, remembering how at the slightest crisis members of the Vancouver commune used to fall into each other's arms. She would like to collapse on Paul right now.

Faye stood near the couch, carefully reading the posters Jeanie had taped on the wall. There was a set of slogans about the present crisis and some photographs of women athletes. Faye shook her head with a slow smile of wonderment. "Jeanette, you must come back to the fold. We all—"

"It's much too late for that," Jeanie said.

"Eli needs you back—"

"He can't have her back!" Paul grabbed Jeanie by the waist, startling her. "I've got her now."

For the first time the smile dropped from Faye's lips. "My father will be very upset," she said. "I promised I would bring you back, at least for a visit. He has little charity for you now."

Little charity. Jeanie straightened out of Paul's embrace. "What did Dennis mean by showing up at Leelannee's school today?" she asked. "I don't want him bothering her. If he wants to see her we can get a lawyer and work out some kind of agreement."

Faye smiled. "I don't understand why you send her to that A-B-C school. Do they teach her biorhythm there? Do they develop her intuition? Will she learn to journey . . ."

"I don't want him bothering her," Jeanie said.

"Then perhaps"—Faye stepped closer, speaking so the followers on the couch would not hear her—"it's time to return Eli's letters and my father's letters. They are too explosive for you to handle. You make dangerous errors of interpretation.

And then you spread false rumors that feed on the ignorance of outsiders."

"I don't have any letters," Jeanie said.

Faye's rings glittered as her fingers flew about the air as if searching for vibrations from the hidden parts of the room. "I can sense that they're not in this apartment. Jeanette, this is meant in full seriousness, you must return them to me."

Jeanie had the feeling that Faye was mentally fingering everything in her drawers and closets. It was even more intrusive than the feet of the followers stepping on her black and white abstract rug. She stood up, ready now to push them out by force if necessary. "I don't know what you want, Faye. The only souvenir I have from Vancouver is Eli's painting." She pointed to the window shade rolled up near the wall. "You can take that with you if you want."

Faye's smile seemed to crack in pieces. "I'm not talking about the painting. You understand my meaning." She walked to the rocker and picked up her purse. "Would you get the car, Thomas?"

"Your wish is my command," he said, stuffing the needlepoint back in his pocket and hurrying down the hall.

"Oh, you really say that," Paul said.

Faye smiled at him. "Of course we do. The words are very important. First comes the word, then the feeling."

Jeanie leaned against the wall, letting Paul wrap up the visit, keeping all thoughts about the letters from her mind as if she was afraid that Faye could read it.

"Why should it make you feel good to say 'Your wish is my command'?" Paul asked.

"Carla can answer that."

The girl turned pink and expanded her cheeks in a wider smile. "When the will is surrendered there is a great sense of freedom. Of peace. A joyous feeling."

"That's the truth," Faye smiled.

Paul's lips formed an O as he nodded as her. "Is that what made you join?"

The girl touched his arm. "The joyous feeling. Yes. When the will is not surrendered there is unhappiness. A sense of loss. Now I'm found. I'm always full."

Faye gave Jeanie a quick hug. "Our spheres will touch again very soon." Then she turned to Paul. "You're a lucky man. Your friend Jeanette is a very special person. You may not be aware of how special. She was one of the original inspirers of a movement that now encircles the globe with its fragrance. And you're very nice too," she added, and was gone.

Paul flopped on the bed as soon as he heard Jeanie clicking the locks. He extended an arm to her, but she stood huddled in the doorway waiting for her body to regain its balance. Paul reached up to turn off the overhead light and lit a cigarette. "That was very heavy," he said finally. "What does she want from you? Letters?"

"I'm going to have to move," Jeanie said. "And it's too bad. I really love this neighborhood."

Paul dragged deeply on the cigarette. "I don't know what you like about this neighborhood. Everyone's over seventy. Do you think she's gonna come back?"

"They've been following me all day in a car. I think I'll be in a safer position once the documents are made public, but who knows? Maybe Eddie Market won't be interested. Maybe it'll have no impact."

"Come here," Paul said, and she moved near the bed and sat down on the floor. He rubbed the back of her neck. "Why didn't you tell me you were involved with those people?"

She laughed. "I was trying not to be involved with them. To forget I ever heard of them. That's why I spend a lot of time with Gail and the coalition against the crisis—at least it has something to do with everyday life. But then when the Church of All invaded the city on this urban crusade and people around the coalition began to say they were being brought in by the government . . ."

"Oh, but that's not true, surely," Paul said. "They have nothing to do with the government. Just a bunch of people standing on the street corner wishing the world a nice day."

Jeanie smiled up at him. Her eyes were getting used to the dark. "You were great. You really helped me out. Tomorrow will be a lot easier on me if you come along."

His cigarette had burned a long ash and he dropped it in the tray she held for him. "Maybe you should just forget about your plans for tomorrow. We could drive out to the ocean and buy some fried shrimps for lunch and maybe go to the movies in the evening."

"Paul, I'm really decided on this. I've been thinking about it for a long time. You're mad, aren't you?"

"No, I just think if you're really finished with your husband and that whole way of life you wouldn't care about taking some kind of revenge on them. You'd just walk away. With me."

"I have some kind of obligation to tell other people what I know," Jeanie said quietly. "Then I can walk away."

He lit another cigarette, and she was annoyed to see him smoke so much, but said nothing. "I thought you might end up leaving with her tonight," he said.

"You did?" She sat on the bed and watched him closely. "No, no, you don't understand, I'm through with all of them. The day the U.S. withdrew from Vietnam I took Leelannee and headed for New York. I was ready for the real world again." She hesitated a moment, then lay down on his heaving chest. "I wish I had told you before, from the beginning. It's just I never thought you'd hang around this long."

His arm circled around her shoulder. "I'm still here. I just think you should let the city worry about how to clear the weirdos off the streets. Let the mayor worry, let the president worry, that's what we pay them for, that's why we let them steal our money. You and I are too busy falling in love and eating hamburgers and going to the movies to worry about this bullshit."

She leaned against him, soothed by the talk, enjoying the lull. "I'll make a deal with you," she murmured. "You come with me tomorrow, and after that I'll follow you around."

He put out his cigarette and they lay quietly in the dark. After a while she was aware of his even breathing. Sleep did not come so easily to her. Faye had stirred up unexpected feelings. She had prepared for the dangers, for the threats, for the tracking. What toppled her composure was the nostalgia she felt for her former self, for that girl so young and naïve that Eli Zinger could wrap her in his dream and give her the joyous feeling of being tightly connected again. Her marriage to Dennis . . . to Brainstorm . . . she couldn't finish her thought. She shook Paul's arm to make sure he was sleeping. Great social changes—that's what she had been after when she let Eli Zinger wrap her in his dream. She had been brought up to expect to change the world. Other parents hid their communism from their children, but hers brought her into the tightly connected circle. The overpowering moral lesson was that you didn't walk away from a fight. Ignorant people could be excused—they didn't always recognize injustice when they saw it. But if you saw it, and you just shrugged your shoulders and walked away . . . that was being like Uncle Leon . . . that was the deadliest sin.

"Let the mayor worry," Paul had said. In her family they

worried for the mayor, for the masses, it was her tradition. "Especially you, Jeanie," her father would tell her. "You have such a high I.Q., you must use it to change things."

She balanced her high I.Q. like a black top hat on her head. She was walking down the street to the first meeting of the Eddie Fisher Fan Club. Miss McElliot had found out Jeanie had a high I.Q. Sally doesn't have a high I.Q. The teacher moved her seat away from Sally next to Mona, Nora, and Patricia, the good girls, the ones who decorated the covers of their book reports with silver glitter to get extra credit. Sally never even did a book report. She couldn't go to the park with Sally because her mother insisted she attend the first meeting of the Eddie Fisher Fan Club.

It was Saturday afternoon! The sun couldn't get in the basement where the girls were sitting on folding chairs around a bridge table. There was a little dish of candy and a plate of cookies so officially placed that Jeanie was afraid to take any. Maybe they were wax cookies.

Mona had a thick envelope from the National Eddie Fisher Fan Club. She read the latest news about Eddie and Debbie and their new home in Beverly Hills. Then she read the instructions for organizing your very own Eddie Fisher Fan Club, which seemed to hinge around the election of officers. It took a long time. Mona was elected president; Nora was vice president; Patricia was secretary. Mona asked Jeanie if she wanted to be Sunshine Girl. "The Sunshine Girl sends birthday cards to all the members and get-well cards when they're sick. . . ."

Jeanie's shirt stuck to the back of the folding chair.

"Well, say something, Jeanie, do you want to be Sunshine girl?"

Those girls could really sit still a long time and talk quietly, one at a time. "You really like Eddie Fisher, huh?" Jeanie said.

"Of course we like him," Patricia said. "We wouldn't be starting this fan club if we didn't like him, would we?"

"And you really like his records, huh?" Jeanie was afraid if she agreed to be Sunshine Girl she'd lose all the Saturday afternoons in the park for the rest of her life. "And you really think he's so cute and all?" She didn't see it. She didn't even think Debbie was pretty.

The other girls were quiet, folding their hands on the table. It was a lesson on how to wear the big top hat of her high I.Q. As soon as I leave, Jeanie thought, I bet they start playing and shouting again like regular kids.

"After the meeting we'll have cokes and listen to some Eddie Fisher records," Mona said. "I have autographed pictures and membership cards. Oh—we should talk about dues."

Jeanie's right leg fell asleep. When she pulled up her sock the needles in her foot made her want to hop and scream. She wanted to get home. The late afternoon shadows were already crossing out the park, but at least she could get home in time to meet Aunt Claire's boyfriend.

Aunt Claire was getting married. Mother knew Leon from summer camp. "She says he's in the party," Mother told Father. *In the party*. The lowered voice, the intimacy, the reverence with which those words were always said. It made her catch her breath until she felt she'd burst with the dream of a just society.

"I heard he was a Browderite," Father said.

Mother shrugged. "Would Claire know the difference?"

Jeanie went to sit on the bed in Evan's room, hoping Mother wouldn't ask her about the Eddie Fisher Fan Club. She opened the Mickey Spillane paperback she'd stolen from the Sweet Shoppe. The first lines got her: "She opened the door. She was as naked as a noodle." Jeanie wondered what Mona, Nora, and Patricia would say about that? You know girls, when Eddie Fisher came home from work the other day Debbie opened the door as naked as a noodle.

Evan was running around the room acting out a baseball game with a rolled up pair of socks. He announced the game as he went. "It's a belching ball to the outfield. It's going . . . going . . . that ball is going . . . foul!"

Claire knocked on the door and brought Leon in. Jeanie jammed the book under the mattress. Leon was skinny and wore glasses. He caught the socks and threw them back to Evan.

"Who ya for?" Evan asked.

"Yankees," said Leon.

Claire groaned. "I should've warned you not to admit it."

Evan jumped up on the bed to glare at Leon on eye level. "We're Dodger fans. But the Yankees are okay this week. Grandpa has them in the pool. For *low*."

"Aw, why do you root for those bums?" Leon laughed. "They'll never get out of the cellar."

"This family always roots for the underdog," Jeanie told him.

Evan brought his collection of baseball cards to the dinner table, stacked them near his plate, and all through dinner showed Leon pictures of Yankee players with their faces inked out.

Jeanie loved the deep blue tablecloth mother had put out. The dishes and glasses looked nice. Aunt Claire was wearing a polka-dot dress—navy with white dots—with a flare skirt. The family sat along the table like the pipes of a mouth organ in graduated sizes, speaking uncommonly soft so that the roar of the passing trains was dominant. Grandma and Grandpa arrived dressed up for the occasion, but after a few minutes Grandpa's jacket and tie hung on the back of his chair, and Grandma went to the bedroom to take off her girdle and put on the slippers she brought in a plastic shopping bag. Father, who was working the night shift, faced the meat and potatoes with a shudder. "Breakfast," he said.

"I hope Leon knows what he's getting into," Mother said, winking at Grandpa.

"Ahh, yeah," said Grandpa, "Claire has been in trouble since kindergarten."

"It's quite a distinction," Mother said. "How many girls played hookey from kindergarten?"

"Evelyn," Claire said. "Not in front of the kids."

"And in junior high," Mother laughed, "she went to 109, Leon, the all-girls junior high. . . ."

"They never told me a thing about it," Grandpa said. "I pick up the paper and there's a picture of Claire picketing the school."

Jeanie tingled to attention. She had heard of picketing shops and government buildings, but schools?

"I hated that school," Claire said. "They made us wear long black lisle stockings—even when it was warm out. They were so hot and itchy and ugly."

Grandpa smoothed down the strand of hair that stretched across his baldness. "In those days anything could happen."

"Claire organized all the girls to wear white anklets to school," Mother said. "Anklets in those days were really risqué. Knee socks were a little daring."

"There were these Young Pioneers in my class," Claire explained. "They were always trying to get me to come to meetings. So I said, let's do something about these awful stockings. So we talked it up. . . ."

"I saw her picture in the paper," Grandpa said.

Jeanie burned with desire to be Claire, to be wearing a blue and white polka-dot dress and go to school in the days when anything could happen, and there were so many different ways of fighting back. She bet Claire never got pushed into going to an Eddie Fisher Fan Club, but then Leon said: "And I thought I was marrying the champion lindy-hopper of the Savoy ballroom."

"That too, that too," Mother laughed.

"We've come a long way since the depression," Leon said.

There was a nod around the table and a silence.

"I don't know if the party's changed any, but the rest of the country certainly has," Leon went on.

The nodding stopped, but the silence continued.

"It's the same old story with the left," Leon said. "Meetings on folding chairs that collapse and one loudmouth consulting his Lenin for the perfect quotation to move the discussion forward, and young girls collecting money about a lynching in the South, and a strike in Pennsylvania, and before you leave, comrades, one more thing, don't forget the revolution is scheduled for Tuesday and it's important for everyone to be on time."

Father and Mother smiled slightly, but Jeanie was alert to the provocation. The hairs on her arm rose with static electricity.

"I can't figure them since they dumped Browder," Leon continued.

Jeanie noted that Leon referred to the party as them, not us. She hadn't known that could happen. She knew Marble-Eyed Maguire hated communists, and Joe McCarthy and the F.B.I. were after them, but this was something new. This was someone who had stood close enough to see the true nature of class society and deliberately turned away.

"I think Browder was okay," Leon said. "He understood that America is not Europe, is not Russia. When times are good the American worker is riding high and the almighty buck is a lot easier to grasp than class solidarity."

Father's face reached a deep red before he spoke. "It's because of your friend Browder that the party's as small as it is today."

"I'm not saying Browder didn't make mistakes, but he understood that when a guy has a good job and is making good money . . ."

"And about lynchings in Alabama and strikes in Pennsylvania," Father's voice roared higher, "those twenty-five-cent contributions . . ."

". . . he's not going to risk it for some pipe dream of a revolution."

". . . victory and defeat for a hell of a lot of people who'd do the same for you." Mother tapped Father's shoulder and he made an effort to lower his voice. Both he and Leon were standing now, facing each other across the table. Jeanie was sparkling with excitement.

"This is a *family*," Grandpa said, his hand on his heart, crumpling his white shirt.

"You feel okay, Sam?" Grandma rummaged in her pocketbook and set his pill bottle on the table.

Father and Leon lowered back into their seats. "The trouble with you, Jay," Leon smiled, "is you got this prolier-than-thou attitude."

Jay tapped his fork against the side of the plate. "You'll go far, Leon. You talk like a boss already."

"Leon." Claire pulled him from the table. "I want to show you Evelyn's drapes in the bedroom. . . ." She hauled him away for a few minutes and Mother sighed. Jay kept tapping his fork. Jeanie's heart was full of power. It was so good to be wrapped in their excitement, in the importance of their words. Grandpa let his breath seep out slowly through loosened lips.

"He's a Yankee fan," said Evan in wonderment, and even Father laughed.

7

Leelannee crawled into bed between her mother and Paul. She gave Paul a good shove to get more room but he didn't move. She pushed her face against her mother's and started sucking her thumb, pushing it rhythmically against the roof of her mouth. Bars of sunlight moved across the ceiling. She gave Paul a good kick and he jerked his leg away and turned over, shaking the whole room. Why did her mother want to sleep with that big thing taking up the whole bed? She pushed her face against her mother's warm neck.

Jeanie's hand groped over the small face. "Go back to bed, Lee."

"Can I have some cereal, Mommy? Just get me some cereal and go back to sleep. Put on the television and you can go back to sleep. I promise."

"It's not time to get up yet! Git!"

Leelannee climbed right over Paul's shoulders and went to sit on the couch. Jeanie's eyes were still closed. She reached for Paul's bare back, feeling the patchwork of warm and cool parts. She rubbed her cheek against his skin. He was still there. She was getting quite a habit. She kissed along the top of his spine, running her fingers through his hair. "Good morning," she said, moving her hands down the curve of his behind, opening her eyes to pull up the covers, and spotting Leelannee on the couch staring at her.

"I want cereal," Leelannee said quickly, before her mother could close her eyes again.

"Mmmm."

Paul was harder to wake up than anyone she'd ever known. He said, "Getting right up," in a clear, assured tone but he slept on.

Jeanie got out of bed to take care of Lee. It was the first free day she'd ever wished she was going to work. In light of today's task even the ring of the cash register seemed gay. And the fooling around during lunch hour on the vast upper floor where Mirrormart kept its stock. Justino pretending his price marker was a gun, and Gail holding forth about building a base among the working class on a real soapbox. It had its charms. She didn't like what she had to do today. But it was necessary. And that isn't only my opinion, she reminded herself. Justino and Gail thought it necessary too. But for them it was a matter of principles, and for her it was a betrayal, not only of Eli and Faye and Brainstorm, but of the girl she once was.

Jeanie brushed Leelannee's hair, adjusting her chin after every stroke. She felt the same tender regard for her former self as she felt for her child. She let herself ride out the sorrow, which came as a gentle rocking motion. Then she brushed Lee's bangs off her forehead and kissed her cool skin. The child will live in the future I create, she thought. I cannot pretend the Church of All is harmless when I *know*. If fascism ever comes to America it will wear not military boots but a smile as ingenuous and pure as the Allees on the corner selling mirrors to examine your eyes.

"Paul! Get up!" She jumped on him and began to bounce. "I'm going to drink the last cup of coffee if you don't hurry." He turned and toppled her, pinning her legs beneath his own.

"I'm going to sleep for a hundred years."

"Come on." She tried to push his legs off her. "I've got so much to do today."

"All right. Put a lot of milk in my coffee. I need the strength. We're gonna change the whole damn world today."

She wiggled off the bed and straightened her skirt. "Come on, drink your coffee while I put my makeup on."

"Who we seeing first? The mayor? The secretary of state?"

"Don't make fun of me," she said. "I think I'm taking a balanced view. I'm not making it more important than it is."

"If I took you seriously . . ." he said. He sat up and drank the coffee.

She was in the bathroom drawing a tremulous line across her eyelid. He came to watch, still undressed. "If I took you seriously . . ."

"Oh, take me any way you want," she said, "just take me." She put her hands on her hips and pouted.

"Ohh, don't do *that*," he said. "Don't ever do that."

"What?"

He put his hands on his hips and stuck his lower lip out. "That."

She flushed, then smiled and kissed his cheek a hundred times until he shook her off in disgust. "You're so bad at flirting," he said. "My ex-wife was good at it and even so I hated it."

"So how'm I supposed to act?"

"Natural, act natural."

She steered him toward his clothes. "That's easy to say, just act natural, just be yourself, whoever the hell that is."

"You've got a pretty strong self. You just keep swallowing it."

Jeanie handed him his jacket. "If I said to you all the things I swallowed you'd be long gone."

He let his jacket drag on the floor. "No, don't say that. Look, what have we been talking about for a month?"

Jeanie was standing holding the hall door open waiting for Paul, who looked like he would fall back on the bed for another hour's sleep just as soon as he finished making his point.

"I've known you for a month . . ."

"Five weeks, three days."

"And I got the impression you were just a normal woman

working to support her kid, maybe going to a few meetings around this crisis situation, but all the time you had these crazy plans running around in your head."

"No. When I was with you I forgot about everything." She urged him into his coat. "You were my vacation."

He leaned against the staircase while she locked the door. "It's not fair."

"It's not fair," Leelannee agreed. "I *never* get to watch television in the morning. Popeye the sailor man is on in the morning."

Jeanie felt a headache land like a beret on top of her scalp. She shook her head and the red/brown curls bounced annoyingly around her face. "All this heavy stuff is coming down and all you're worried about is our relationship."

"Our relationship . . ."

The door across the hall opened and Mrs. Feldman stuck her head out. Jeanie gulped at being caught in the hall so early with a man.

"Is your buzzer broken, dear?" Mrs. Feldman asked.

"I guess so. Isn't everyone's?"

"Last night there was a man, a strange type, bald as a bean, ringing your buzzer. And when I went down for rolls just now I saw him sitting out front in his car. Isn't that strange?"

"What kind of a car?"

"Big and green."

Paul sucked in his breath and folded his arms across his chest. Leelannee pulled on her mother, gesturing toward Mrs. Feldman's apartment. She could see the antique gold satin furniture in the living room. She thought it was so interesting to see other people's apartments and find they were not furnished like her mother's.

"The thing to do," Jeanie said, "is call the police and tell them someone is loitering near the building."

Mrs. Feldman nodded and closed the door.

"She'll do it too," Jeanie said to Paul. "She's great about that. She's the one who always calls the department of health when the compactor breaks and insists on leaving her name." She hurried them into the elevator and rang the basement button. "Where's your car, Paul?"

"A few blocks down. Wallace."

"Do you think you can drive around and pick us up and not go by the man sitting in the big green car out front?"

He nodded. "Cops and robbers."

"Dum de dum dum."

"Scared?"

She looked at her trembling arms. "Why, yes."

"I'm glad you're that much in touch with reality."

Jeanie and Leelannee waited near the basement door, looking out the wired window at the chunks of garbage that had been tossed about the streets by last night's wind. Leelannee tried to wiggle her finger into the crack along the glass until Jeanie slapped her hand away. She felt a pride that Mrs. Feldman had spotted the green Chrysler. Her neighbors were protecting her, they were on their toes. It was a connected feeling, the kind she had in the projects when she was a kid before it all fell apart, before her parents moved up up up to Avocado Towers where the neighbors wouldn't find you if you lay bleeding in the hall.

"Hey!" Leelannee wailed, "you forgot my lunch box."

"No school today, honey. You're going to play at Gail's for a little while."

"Is it Saturday?"

Jeanie traced the child's apple cheeks with her fingers. "It's a holiday."

"Are you gonna stay at Gail's too? I don't want to go to Gail's. I want to go to Grandma's."

"Grandma's working."

"But it's a holiday. Are you working today?"

"No."

"How come? Cause it's a holiday? What holiday is it? Is it Christmas, I mean Hanukkah? Ma!"

Jeanie saw Paul's white convertible pull alongside the building and she rushed Leelannee into the car. The sun gleamed off the dusty windshield. "Did you see a big green car in front of the house?" she asked.

"How could I? I didn't go that way." They both looked out the back window but the only motion was a blue compact car pulling out of a parking spot at the end of the block, so they drove toward the parkway with Jeanie's head resting on Paul's shoulder and Leelannee jumping up and down in the back seat.

The blue compact car hung back, letting a car remain between him and Paul's. A needlepoint canvas lay open on the seat beside the driver, Thomas Baker, who glanced at it occasionally. He had trouble keeping out of sight once the white convertible left the parkway and curved around the bumpy streets of City Island. When he saw the dead end sign on the final block he didn't turn in, but parked behind a gas station and walked into the block. As soon as he saw which house the white convertible pulled into, Thomas hurried back to the car, running with his arms bent at the elbow and his fists loosely clenched. He called Faye Zinger on the car radio.

"How *are* you," she asked, after taking down the information. "Your orbit was wobbly last night."

Thomas leaned his cheek against the cold glass of the car window. He sat facing a pile of junked cars and oil drums. "The outside is getting to me," he told Faye, and he had to repeat it twice to make himself understood over the static of the car radio. He had joined All to be inside, but since the Urban Crusade began he'd been pulling outside assignments. Faye murmured, then shouted her sympathy. She promised to have a word with Cordite. She told him to think about the higher purposes of their work. When the call was over Thomas left the metal sanctuary of the car for the unfriendly territory of the outside.

8

Gail Macellancy's house was really a summer bungalow that had been insulated, heated, and rented for year round use. It was in a row of four bungalows, one in front of the other, in a line that slouched toward the sea wall. Leelannee ran ahead of Jeanie and Paul, making a wide circle around the big dog chained to the gate of the first house, and banged on Gail's door. Leelannee believed that Gail lived in a doll's house, and the white ruffled curtains and checked linoleum in the three tiny rooms proved it. Gail had a mother cat and two kittens living under her wicker couch. Gail let her go in and out, out and in, as often as she liked without even asking. Gail was on the telephone most of the time and didn't care so much what kids did.

By the time Jeanie and Paul entered the cottage, Leelannee was poking her head in Gail's refrigerator for a can of orange soda. Gail was on the telephone and just waved hello. Jeanie picked around the house, glancing at the draft leaflet on the kitchen table:

> The folks who brought you Vietnam and Watergate now present *THE CRISIS*, a new and alarming method of cutting back on your standard of living while increasing profits at the top.

The signature on the bottom said: *Put out by the workers' coalition . . . we'd rather fight than bitch.* The leaflet was crayoned on bits of paper, slashed together, reworked. At least it wasn't the old 1930s' rhetoric. It was the new rhetoric, Jeanie thought with a smile. She picked up a pencil and wrote *labor donated* on the bottom of the sheet. The daughter of a printer, she never forgot to look for the union bug when someone handed her a leaflet. She was half listening to Gail telling someone how important it was to attend the mounting series of protests against the crisis price hikes.

"You gotta come, George, and bring all the boys in the shop out with you. What are you, dead and buried? I've seen more fight in an overcooked stringbean."

"A stringbean!" howled Leelannee, shakily pouring orange soda into the plastic Wonder Woman cup Gail kept for her young visitors.

Gail was laughing too. "Okay, George, I'm sorry, I just been making twenty-three phone calls and this is my day off. I know it's not easy to get people mobilized these days. But there must be one or two people in the shop you can talk to."

Jeanie noticed Gail had lumps gathering around her thighs, stretching her jeans. All the delicatessen lunches and cupcake dinners gulped at meetings were showing on her neglected body. The women had gone to high school together, and Jeanie felt the signs of aging in her friend were like a shadow across her own youth. Of course Jeanie was still thin. Even a year after leaving All she still had a distaste for packaged, air-fluffed foods and was too nervous to eat much at all. Maybe the nervousness would go away soon. When she handed Eddie Market the documents she'd be free of all former feelings, free to make choices without the burden of old mistakes, free to get fat and rot her teeth and enjoy life.

Paul leaned against the window, looking out on the winter lawn. Jeanie thought he was shutting himself off from the political slogans that leaped around the bungalow. On her lampshade Gail had a collection of historical buttons, dating back to BAN THE BOMB and WE SHALL OVERCOME, up to the pin from a basketball tournament she had attended on a prelegal visit to the People's Republic of China. Her bookshelf was packed with those yellow-covered Mao, Marx, and Lenin pamphlets that Jeanie remembered her mother packing in cartons to store in the project's bicycle room during the McCarthy investigations. Paul was from a different sort of background. He'd been taught to leave well enough alone. To drink at the same watering hole as the bosses and mobsters and avoid a clash of horns. Ideological pain. But maybe it was just as well she was with a guy like Paul. Brainstorm, with his left-wing scientist of a father, had brought her worse pain.

Gail put down the phone at last, threw her arms around Jeanie, and sobbed mock tears on her shoulder. "I can't wait until this damn demo is over and I can just . . . you know I haven't been to bed with Jake in weeks. Hi, Paul."

Paul smiled and nodded, then turned back to the window.

"See something out there?" Gail asked.

"Just dogs and cats," Paul said, but he kept his watch.

"So," Gail turned back to Jeanie with her eyebrows raised in peaks of expectancy. "This is your big day."

"I can't wait until it's over," Jeanie said. "I hope we'll be back for Leelannee by three, but it's very hard to say."

"It's okay." Gail tossed a bag of chips into Lee's lap. "I'll just wait in for you. Jake should be home by noon. You're the important one today. Oh, it's so exciting."

"Yeah, it's a real thrill," Paul tossed over his shoulder.

"I'm not thrilled and I'm not excited," Jeanie said. She walked over to the papier-mâché framed mirror on the bathroom door. "I just hope if Eddie Market puts me on television that I look decent and convincing, not like some wild-eyed chick on a vendetta because Eli Zinger stopped sleeping with her."

"You," Gail snorted. "You look like you just got out of high school."

"I saw Faye Zinger last night," Jeanie said, "and she looked so old and knocked out. . . ."

Gail didn't recognize the name right away. She and Jeanie had endlessly discussed the Church of All, but mostly in terms of its social effects, its political meaning. They seldom referred to the personalities Jeanie had been wrapped up with. "Is that Zinger's wife?" Gail asked.

"Wife number one," Jeanie laughed. "Yes, she dropped by to pay us a little visit last night. Very unpleasant."

"I don't like it," Gail said. "How did she know?"

"How did she know where I lived, what I was planning to do, that I had documents hidden somewhere? Either someone in the coalition is an agent, or someone at Eddie Market's office . . . or it's you or me." Jeanie was still looking in the mirror, brushing her red curls away from her face, trying out earnest middle-class expressions to use on Eddie Market.

"It's not you or me." Gail smiled. "I think you should have people stay with you today. Justino called in sick too . . . the manager must be having a fit. Why don't I get him to round up some—"

"No, don't," Paul and Jeanie said together.

"We made a decision on this, we have to stick to it," Jeanie said. "They're not going to accost me in the street. I know that group. They're just not that dangerous."

Gail sat on the edge of the kitchen table, hand poised over the phone. "When we made that decision we didn't think they'd be following you."

Jeanie fingered her eyelids to even out her makeup. "I don't want to distract a lot of people from building the demonstration. This exposé is just a minor part of it, right? And it's my responsibility."

"Let's go," Paul said, pushing himself away from the window.

"I think you could use more protection," Gail insisted. "They're not harmless and you know it."

Jeanie put her arm on her shoulder. Gail stared at her with such intensity that it made her smile. "You're going to make me chicken out. Let's not make this more complicated than it already is. Take care of Leelannee, take care of mounting a good demonstration. That will be my best protection."

Gail started to pick up the phone. "At least let's talk to Justino and some of the others about it."

"No." Jeanie shook with annoyance. "We made a decision, I can't stand to go over it all again. We can't control everything. The other side always makes moves you don't expect."

"The circumstances have changed," Gail began. But Paul had opened the door to the bungalow and Jeanie leaned down to kiss Leelannee, who began to cry. Then the gray kitten ran over Lee's feet and she stopped crying and crawled under the couch after it.

"Don't worry," Jeanie said. "Remember, I'm a third generation red–I'm not so new at this."

"Call and let me know what Market says," Gail said. "When you get to the loft talk to Justino . . . maybe he'll be able to come. . . ." The phone rang and Paul pulled Jeanie out of the house before the two women could start up again.

"My God," he said, "she acts like she's your mother."

Jeanie nodded. She felt elated to be free of her child, on her way to tossing out the secrets that had been nagging at her for over a year. She put her arm through his as they walked toward his white convertible. "Gail worries about me a lot. But she helps too. When I first left All she helped me find an apartment and got me a job at Mirrormart."

"That was some favor," Paul said. "Three twenty-five an hour."

"But where else," Jeanie said, "would I get to work with a half-dozen radicals who took working-class jobs so they could build a revolutionary movement? I felt isolated enough after leaving All. At least at work I have friends."

She got in the car and leaned across to open Paul's door, which had a broken lock. "If I had gone to college, I would never take a job like yours," Paul said.

He swerved into a gas station a block away from Gail's and got out, spending quite a while fiddling under the hood. Jeanie got out and went to the ladies' room, passing the blue compact car that was parked at the back of the station. She spent as long as she could in the ladies' room, but when she came back Paul was still working on the car. "Do you have to do that *now*?" she said.

He nodded, without looking up. She stood beside him a while, staring at the engine without comprehension. She could feel Gail's apprehension plating her mind. The situation *had* changed. The coalition had carefully mapped plans for what to do when the Church of All began to defend itself, but no one had raised the possibility that they might take action before she even gave Eddie Market the documents. Standing there in the gas station she imagined sniper rifles peeking out of the winter trees. If she were killed Brainstorm would get Leelannee. Lee would grow up with a gold disc on her shirt, chanting obedience to false gods. "Paul! What are you doing? I told Eddie Market I'd be there *early*, and we have to get the stuff at the loft first."

As soon as she'd said it she was sorry. Was someone listening in the high bushes? The sky had an eggshell color.

The pebbles on the ground were distinct, important. She was shaking at the shoulders.

"Get in the car," Paul said, "you're cold."

He took so long putting in the gas and talking to the station owner that Jeanie began to wonder if Paul was the agent. Perhaps he'd been assigned to keep her from unburdening her secrets today. No. He couldn't have told Zinger what she was planning to do. He didn't know himself until last night.

Finally he got in the car and turned on the engine, smiling. "There, that wasn't too bad, was it?" He looked at her, shaking his head. "You look like you're gonna pass out. You know, babe, you can just forget this whole thing. We can go get a six-pack and drive around to the dock where I work . . . I'd love to show you off to some of the guys. . . ."

"Let's go downtown. West Side," she said.

His hands remained resting on his thighs. "Are you sure you're feeling—"

"Paul. Honey." She felt ready to jump from the car. "Could you at least drive me to the subway?"

He sighed and moved the car into gear. "You know something?" he said. "I don't really understand what's going on."

Jeanie turned on the radio. "Just think of it as a couple of errands I have to get done before we can go for that six-pack." She listened hard to the hit parade tunes, the ads, the record package from the Sensational Sixties. It came as a slight surprise to her that the sixties were already history, subject to nostalgia.

"What did you do during the sensational sixties?" she asked Paul, after a long silence.

"I must have been behind the times," he shrugged. "I didn't even notice that they were sensational."

"Oh, I think they were," Jeanie said. "Anything could

happen then, and did. Too bad I blew it and ended up in All."

She was waiting for some kind of revelation from him: for his opinions on hippies, the Vietnam War, drugs, and Zen Buddhism. She wanted to know him instantly, to be assured that in some general way he was on her side, even if he didn't have a clear idea of what was going on. She lowered the radio and directed him through a maze of intercrossing highways. They both looked frequently out of the back window, but everything always seemed normal.

She settled back against the fraying upholstery, half closing her eyes. It bothered her that Gail was so concerned. Gail didn't panic easily. If she was alarmed about Faye's visit, perhaps Jeanie wasn't taking it seriously enough. Gail had fairly good judgment, even if she did sometimes act as if making revolution was a brand new idea she'd just thought up.

A song floated up from the radio and Jeanie found herself humming it before she was aware of the words. Then she stopped humming and listened. "Soft, slow surrender. Love, live without fear. Like a dream in the evening. Like a cloud in the air."

"That's a reactionary lyric," she said to Paul, but the song was over and she had to repeat it for him.

"Very reactionary," he agreed.

"It could be the theme song of the Church of All."

"It could be my theme song," he said, looking straight ahead and smiling. "What am I doing now if not surrendering to you?"

She looked out the window at the wrinkled surface of the Hudson River. Along the shore huge cranes swung building materials over the water. She didn't like what Paul had said, though she imagined it was true. He might be driving the car but she was in control, choosing the direction, commanding the speed. She was grateful that he allowed room for pauses and things left unexplained, that he was willing to go along for the ride. With Brainstorm each decision had been debated with such endless passion that they usually changed sides several times before she gave up in exhaustion. Paul gave her time to clear her head. She couldn't afford to lose direction now. She had to steer carefully and stay in control of that part of her life which she did rule. She had to be ready for the unexpected. She thought of the time the pedals had spun out of control under her, the day she lost the belief that she alone commanded her destiny.

She had a light bike, a powder-blue Higgins, not the clattery Schwinns that most kids had. She was eleven years old when she learned to ride it. She rode in the park, on the bicycle path, where the river had flooded and withdrawn, leaving a washerboard of gray mud. She curved perfectly between the rail and the stone wall around the first bend of the underpass. Around the second bend she saw them.

His hips pinned her straight black skirt against the railing. She was bent back over the rail, her head dangling toward the water, pins falling from her hair at every slap. She was naked on top. Her breasts rose and fell like slightly deflated balloons as he slapped and slapped her face. Her head fell from one shoulder to another. He reached down one time to slap her breasts which floated up from the impact. Her mouth was open as her head rolled and her cloud-colored breasts wavered with each slap.

They didn't look at Jeanie. She rode the Higgins around the next curve and out alongside the river. So that was what *it* was like. You just ride around a curve and there's sex slapping you in the face. She pedaled the Higgins faster and faster, gripping the rubber on the handle bars until it dug lines into her palms. The trees blurred by and the benches and then that one bad hill in the park, the one she never rode down but walked to the bottom and watched the boys do it. There was hot smoke in her chest. The bike was going faster than ever and this time she was going to ride down the hill. She steered clear of the low fence. She went down the steep black path, thinking she was making it, until the pedals spun out of control and banged against her ankle. When the curve came up she pulled the handle bars and fell, very slowly, lazily, into the ditch of damp branches and stinging weeds.

She was scratched all over. There was blood on the surface of her legs, but it was not flowing. The smoke had not been blown out of her chest; it still ached. The fender of the Higgins was bent into the tire, so she had to walk it home in wet dungarees and grass-stained shirt, her father's shirt with white tails flapping at her knees.

She dragged the bike into the lobby of her building. The smoke thickened in her chest. The two men were there again. Of all the times for *them* to appear. Just what she needed. Two men in highly polished black shoes. Look at the shoes, her father said. New Yorkers never have their shoes polished unless they're cops.

Or going to a funeral, Mother joked, holding Evan's attention as best she could though he was squirming and looking every which way.

The men came over to Jeanie. One tall, blond, with a red face. The other short and bulky. "How are you today, Jeanie?"

You're just a dumb kid, Jeanie, her father said. That's the act. You dunno nuttin'.

"Is your mother home now? Or are you old enough to have your own key?"

The key hung on a string, cold against her chest. They'd never get it from her.

"How'd you wreck your bike?" the other one asked. She

kept her eyes down on the streaked tiles of the lobby floor. The scratches on her face burned.

"Is your father at work today?" His voice was so nice. "I bet you'll be having another one of those meetings at your house tonight. Huh?"

She heard the elevator grinding down.

"We were just going to the candy store to get some ice cream. Want to come along? What's your favorite flavor?"

Vanilla fudge, always vanilla fudge on a sugar cone. They held the door open for her as she dragged her bike into the car. They didn't get in.

Jeanie was going to tell her mother about the underpass. About the slapping and the naked breasts. But she had to tell her about the men in the lobby.

"Those bastards," Mother said, wiping up her scratches. "Did they hurt you? What happened?"

"No, I crashed my bike. Nothing happened."

"Did you tell them anything?"

"No." Mum's the word.

"Good girl," Mother said. She hugged her tight.

"It's because we're communists, huh?"

"It's because they're bastards," her mother said, hugging her tight, sharing but not easing the chewed feeling in her chest. Nothing would ease the feeling. Not Evan crashing into her room to tell her about the new baseball trades. Not the wet, gluey feeling in her panties she could bring on with images of the couple in the park. Not the day her mother sent her out to collect cartons because they were moving out of reach of the shiny black shoes to Avocado Towers where . . .

9

Paul reached over and knocked on Jeanie's forehead. He had just turned onto Nineteenth Street. "Stop dreaming and find me a parking spot."

She let the chewed feeling hang in her chest and found a parking spot between two driveways. Perhaps today would ease her heart. She would steer carefully and not surrender no matter how they slapped her in the face. She would thwart life's tendency of never coming to conclusions.

The freight elevator took them up to the loft in slow, jerky motions. Paul leaned unsteadily against the elevator wall. "I don't like heights," he said. "I don't mind going to the deeps to lay underwater cable, but you couldn't pay me enough to build a high-rise. My father's the same way."

Jeanie put her hand over his. The elevator stopped and the side, rather than the front, door opened. They entered a cubicle facing a wall tacked with mimeographed announcements and a hand-crayoned sign: *Remember to take down the garbage!* There was a roar of noise from a small printing press, the clatter of a mimeograph, shouting and laughter and phones ringing. The loft was a home for young and not so young activists searching for cohesion. They washed up at the loft like debris from the unfinished storms of the sixties' movements: pacifists who were not satisfied by U.S. withdrawal from bomb-pitted Nam; women who divorced and found their liberation illusory; Latins who felt their cause had never come up in the age of rage. They gathered around the issues—lunacy in the White House, crisis-hyped price rises, strikes in the far West that needed support—wondering why the masses of people were simmering at home instead of taking to the streets. They assumed it was just a temporary lull.

A teenage boy moved the curtain aside and buzzed Jeanie in. A long arm waved to them, and a tall man with a curly Afro haircut came toward them through the crowded office.

"Justino, this is Paul," Jeanie said, kissing his cheek. He shook hands with Paul, then led them past the clattering printing machine, stepping carefully around the students painting letters on long banners of red silk, to a small office with stacks of folding chairs and overflowing ashtrays.

"I just spoke to Gail," Justino said, after closing the door. "She's all worried about you."

He had a smile of white teeth against puffy lips that had once made Jeanie open her bedroom door for him. "As you see," she smiled, "we're okay."

He nodded, smiling. "Yes, you're looking very good. If you want I can get a few people to go with you today. But I hate to give them up. With the demo tomorrow, everyone's so busy."

"We don't need any help," Jeanie said. She was stirred with memories of his skin, the color of fine Scotch whiskey. "How's Teresa?" she asked in quick penance.

"She's fine. Next week I'll be a father."

"Hey, Justino," a young voice called over the partition.

"Si?"

"How do you spell *parasite*?"

Jeanie and Justino laughed. "They're writing a leaflet, I take it," she said. Paul was not laughing. He looked like a man impatiently awaiting his wife outside a department store; his eyes were tilted inward.

"The students are very enthusiastic," Justino said. "But you have to proofread carefully. I better go to them." He patted Jeanie's shoulder. "Good luck, compañera."

She nodded and led Paul into another office with a wall of wooden lockers. Most of the square doors were ajar, but one was closed with a combination lock. Jeanie did the combination twice before she was successful. She took out a manila envelope and slid it into her large pocketbook. "Let's go."

In the elevator Jeanie thought of Justino and how he had been against any coalition involvement in the exposé of All. He thought it would blur the issue. He thought it would take up people's time. "If we agree that the Church of All is in town to distract people from their real problems, then how can we let it distract us from ours?" It was a cogent argument and if Jeanie hadn't been so personally involved with All, she might have sided with him. But instead she'd brought in her precious documents to show the group and the majority decision was that she, Gail, and a telephone repairman named Larry should form a subcommittee to bring the information to the public at a strategic moment. Larry had proved little interested in the project, and Gail was always too busy, so Jeanie—with the company of her doubts and hesitancies—thought about it obsessively and alone. Now there was Paul, but as she glanced at him he asked suddenly: "Did you sleep with him?"

"Who?"

"That guy up there."

"Justino? Boy, is it that obvious?"

"I'm asking."

"What difference does it make? I thought we agreed not to get into a blow by blow. . . ."

"I'm *asking* you."

He stood outside the car, waiting for his answer before he opened the door.

"Well," she shrugged, "the answer is obvious."

"What's obvious?"

"Look, if it was no I'd of said it right away, right?"

He unlocked the car door for her and went around to the

other side. She got in, took the manila envelope from her purse, and looked through the sheaf of papers. The letters were all there in slippery Xerox copies. The originals were in her parents' safe deposit box. She started to show them to Paul, but as she looked at him she knew he was only wondering if Justino had a big dick and was good in bed.

"He was terrible," Jeanie said.

Paul tried to keep a straight face, but his smile cracked through. "Liar."

"No, I'm not. We shook hands afterward and decided against a rerun."

"You're a liar," Paul said, "but thanks anyway." He messed with her hair for a moment before he started the engine.

Jeanie turned back to the letters in her lap. She'd been over them hundreds of times before, but each time the meaning and significance seemed to elude her. The Church of All was receiving large sums of government money. That much was clear. Eli Zinger paraded around town like a self-styled revolutionary drawing in lost, discontented people as fast as his organization could absorb them. And all the while he collected money from the Department of Health, Education and Welfare for a drug-abuse program.

She turned to Paul, suddenly excited that very soon she would have the chance to show the letters to Eddie Market.

"What would you think," she said to Paul, "if I told you that Eli Zinger was on the government payroll?"

They were stopped in traffic as a truck backed into a warehouse entrance. Paul glanced at the letter she held up to him. "I must be getting old," he said. "Nothing surprises me in the least any more." Several drivers behind him were leaning on their horns, so Paul gave his a few toots also. Jeanie covered her ears. As they edged around the truck Jeanie saw a coalition poster on top of other peeling papers on the side of a building. The poster said TAKE IT OFF THE TOP! and showed the united arms of brown, white, and yellow people preventing the bony hand of profit from taking money out of their pockets. The simplicity of the poster style made Jeanie a bit uncomfortable, in the same way that her parents cringed at the bad mimeographing on the appeal letters they still got from left-wing causes. But that didn't stop them from sending in a contribution, and it didn't stop Jeanie from putting up the embarrassing posters.

"There's a coalition poster," she said to Paul, who didn't look because the light had turned yellow and he raced the car across the intersection. They were nearing Rockefeller Center and the traffic was extremely heavy. Only a car or two managed to cross the street before the light changed.

"Why don't I sit in the car while you go up?" Paul asked. "We'll never find a spot around here."

"We'll put it in a lot," she said. "The coalition will reimburse me." She tried to think of something else to say, some way to make him feel needed and wanted, but the feeling of anticipation held her attention. She felt as if the tree might really fruit this time, that her meeting with Market could be cathartic, freeing her once and for all from the feeling that her heart was chewed around the edges. She would live up to her own high standards of courage.

She walked a little ahead of Paul as they wound up the curving ramp of the parking into the cold gray air. The streets were full of people hurrying around each other, standing in front of store windows, leaning against cars, slouching in doorways. Two children with paper bags tied around their feet with rubber bands were playing in the street. Jeanie was jostled by three businessmen. In their gray, brown, and blue overcoats they seemed to embody all the possibilities of good taste as they strode by a man in a purple leather jacket who was getting off the bus.

Jeanie paused to let Paul catch up with her. There was an infuriating slowness about his movements today. He put his arm across her shoulder. It felt very heavy. Across the street Jeanie saw a pink-faced boy approaching a pedestrian. He stopped to talk to the boy, who whispered intently, pressing a tract on the man, extending his hand for a contribution.

"There's one," Jeanie pointed out to Paul. "An Allee."

He followed her gaze. "How can you tell?"

"Well, I happen to know that one. But I can usually tell anyway. They seem to wash their faces with sincerity every morning."

As they rounded the corner Jeanie saw a whole squad of Allees on the street. A crowd had gathered around one of the girls who was standing under a banner proclaiming the Urban Crusade. Jeanie tugged on Paul's hand and brought him in closer, until she recognized the girl as Helena Carpenter, the Senator's daughter they'd seen on television. She had a birdlike, darting manner, jerking her elbows out from her sides as she spoke, leading with one shoulder as she stepped near someone in the audience to offer a tract and praise Eli Zinger. After a moment another woman took over. "New York City is in ruins!" she said. The crowd pushed forward a bit to hear her, for she had abandoned her megaphone. "It's time to take the inner journey. We can all transcend together with a sigh, like pollen on the winds of change." She extended her hands in supplication.

"It is windy," someone said. A few people laughed.

"That's the truth," said Helena Carpenter.

"That *is* the truth," said the other Allee. "It's the wind of change." She looked up at the banner which snapped back and forth above her head.

Two women put down their shopping bags to put coins in the plate, shaped like a gold disc, that Helena Carpenter was passing through the crowd. Others backed away.

The Allee took up the megaphone to begin again. "The Church of All Urban Crusade comes at a crucial moment in history. Its attraction is felt by all who recoil from rottenness and sin. Eli Zinger explains it as a lodestar—a star that shows the way toward the journey we must all make toward ourselves. . . ."

Paul kept his eyes in motion to make sure they weren't noticed. Finally he pulled Jeanie away. "Are you sure you're really through with these people? I think they still fascinate you."

Jeanie nodded. "In a way. How did you like her actually saying 'sin.' Eli Zinger used to deny the concept of sin. I guess he's found it useful now. There's still something about them that I don't understand."

"They all say the exact same thing," Paul commented.

"Yeah. It's a trick of theirs. It makes them think in unison."

They entered the ornate lobby of the CRA Building. A flock of tourists was being led around the building by a guide in a maroon coat. Jeanie stopped to let them pass, looking in her wallet for the paper on which she'd written Eddie Market's office number. She didn't have it.

"Great," said Paul.

She looked in her jacket pockets and through her bag once more, getting nervous as the inner wheels seemed to be spinning out of her control. "Well, I'll just have to call him. I memorized his phone number." She had learned to memorize phone numbers years ago when a friend was arrested at an antiwar protest. His address book was confiscated and all his friends received FBI visits, including ex-girlfriends, employers, and out-of-town relatives.

The tourists passed into a large elevator on their way to view a television quiz show. Paul motioned to the drug store across the lobby. "Let's get some coffee."

"All right." Her voice was small. She had lost her piece of paper. She was surrounded by high-stepping women and confident men with briefcases, hurrying in and out of the lobby on missions of great importance. High leather boots, leather gloves, charm bracelets. The women looked like they had just had their hair cut at the same salon. No purple leather jackets here, or children with paper bags tied around their feet. Paul looked as out of place as she, but he didn't appear to notice, swinging his arm around her as they entered the coffee shop.

As soon as he sat down at the counter, Jeanie left to make the call. She used up three dimes. The switchboard operator kept putting her on hold and playing piped music into her ear. This is what hell must be like, Jeanie thought. You try to get in to explain to God why you sinned and the angel at the switchboard keeps putting you on hold. You spend eternity rehearsing what you'll say to Him when you finally get through. At last she reached Eddie Market's secretary, who told her the floor and room number.

By the time she returned Paul was on his second cup of coffee. A woman with gold hoop earrings was smiling at him across the counter, but dropped her eyes before Jeanie's glance. Jeanie drank her cold coffee quickly, standing next to the stool. Then she hurried Paul toward the elevators.

"I feel like I'm going to apply for a job or something," she said.

"This is a very official place." He gestured toward the marble floors, the long directory of names, the elevators that specialized in going to certain floors.

"Yeah, the corridors of power. I'm not used to being inside these places."

"Maybe we should go outside and throw rocks at the windows."

10

Eddie Market set the heels of his Western-style boots on the windowsill and gazed out at the Hudson River, waiting to hear if the woman on the other end of the telephone would say anything new. He had courted Mrs. Carpenter for weeks, but now that she was calling him almost every day at eleven o'clock she was giving him nothing but her outrage. He waited for a pause in her rambling story and said, "Can you tell me about the money?"

"You're not listening to me," she said in a hushed tone. "I've been trying to tell you."

"If you could just give me a more . . . organized story. It doesn't . . ."

She sounded as if she were holding the phone very close to her mouth. "They're always giving me sedatives. That's why I'm not coherent. I'm calling you between nurses."

"I saw Helena this morning," Market prompted. "She was giving out All literature near my office. Has she called you recently?"

"They never let her call. Helena is handicapped, don't you understand? Retarded, they used to call it, before that word went out of style. She's a very pretty girl, but she's not—"

"Look, Mrs. Carpenter, many young people are attracted to that Church these days. And their parents get upset. That's not enough—"

"A half million dollars! That's enough, isn't it? Helena used to be a very rich lady. The Senator could have gone to court. He could legally have prevented her from handing five hundred thousand dollars over to that phony minister."

Market tapped his heels against the glass. "He told the

press he didn't want to violate his daughter's religious freedom. I can buy that." Market knew something about the marginal definitions of mental retardation and thought that if Helena had been born into a less ambitious family she might not have become such an outcast. He was not going to go on the air to say that because Helena Carpenter was an heiress she shouldn't be permitted to turn over all her earthly goods to the Church of All.

"Religious freedom," Mrs. Carpenter laughed softly. "You say you've been investigating this for weeks but you don't have the slightest idea what All is. I thought everyone knew. Everyone on Capitol Hill knows. It's an experiment in social control, as they say. A caretaker agency. Got a problem? Juvenile delinquents? Unemployed youths? Promiscuous young retarded girls? Turn them over to Eli Zinger. He'll amuse them. But in all my life I never thought it would happen to Helena."

"Who else says it's a Washington agency? Who else can I talk to? What about Senator Vallentine?"

"He wouldn't talk to you. I'm the only one crazy enough to talk to Market the Maverick."

Market laughed. He had been called a maverick so many times that he once looked it up in the dictionary and discovered the word derived from Samuel A. Maverick, a nineteenth-century Texan who neglected to brand his cattle. Market was thrilled to be considered unbranded.

"Tell me this. If All is a government agency, where do they get their money?"

Mrs. Carpenter's breathing became more excited. "Helena gave him a half million. Maybe other kids . . ."

Market heard a female voice in the background asking her who she was talking to. "Well, goodbye, Mother," Mrs. Carpenter said. "The nurse is here now. I'll call you tomorrow."

The connection broke. Market took his feet off the windowsill and hung up the phone. He stared at the plaque on his desk on which brass letters spelled DON'T FENCE ME IN. Market was a Midwesterner by birth, but since the maverick title got started his staff began supplying him with cowboy implements on his birthday. He had a rusted branding iron in the corner that his secretary had picked up at an auction when she was camping in Utah.

He leaned over and pushed the button on his intercom. "Dorothy, would you send Ms. Burger in."

Jeanie had ducked into the ladies' room to pull down the blouse that was wiggling out of her skirt. It was a very fancy ladies' room, quite unlike the toilet shed with a cracked mirror that she used at Mirrormart. The walls were pink tile and a long mirror stretched above the pink Formica counter. She dabbed at the eyeliner which had run down the corner of one eye and wondered if she should get her hair clipped shorter in one of the new styles. She was enjoying this glimpse at the inside of a building she had picketed. Market had a reputation as a dissenter, but in these fancy corridors he must often shake the hands of those he criticized.

Eddie Market's office was large, and he walked around the desk to shake her hand. His shirtsleeves were rolled to his elbows, his tie loosened, and he looked like a paler version of his television self. His mustache curled in toward his lips. His eyes were alert and humorous. Jeanie tabulated every detail as she introduced Paul, framing a description for the women at work. She'd have to remember to mention the pink ladies' room.

Jeanie sat in the upholstered chair that Market offered, but shifted it to the side so she could see out the window behind Market's desk. He had a view of the Hudson, where a barge pulled by a tugboat was inching down the silver surface.

Market followed her glance. "Still cold out? I haven't been out since this morning."

"Freezing," Paul answered. "A lot of wind."

"It was so warm yesterday. That's one of the things I like about New York—those unexpected warm days in winter."

Jeanie smiled. "I like that too."

When Market smiled his mustache curled even closer to his lips. "Well, Ms. Burger . . . what made you come to me? Why not the newspapers or . . ."

"I watch your show," she said. It seemed like a dumb reply. She read newspapers too. Market waited, looking more thoughtful than he ever did on TV when he spoke at high speed and punched out question after question. "I like the way you're keeping track of the Church," Jeanie continued. "No one else seems to be making any critical judgments about them. No one else is even noticing how fast they're growing."

Market nodded. "I am very interested in them. And I guess you can say critical."

Jeanie noticed his caution. For all his passionate investigation, she'd always felt he, personally, didn't care too much which way things came out. But Gail said he had been helpful to the coalition during the meat market scandal, despite maintaining a scrupulously unbiased attitude. Jeanie could scarcely imagine a life in which you tried not to take sides. She had been branded from birth, and accepted it as a badge of honor.

"When did you leave the Church?" Market asked.

"When it became a church. A year ago."

"Oh," he looked surprised, tilting back his chair. "So I guess the logical question is, why now?"

"Maybe if they never came to New York I . . . They're all over the place now. I've been doing political work around the crisis and it's so hard to reach people. They're distracted by this Urban Crusade."

Market nodded again. He was not taking notes. "You know you're the first ex-member to come forward."

Jeanie pictured the old movie gag where the army sergeant

asks for volunteers and everyone in the line steps back, leaving a daydreaming soldier as the "volunteer." Had she come forward, or had the Church taken a giant step back?

"What about you, Paul?"

"Me? I was never in it. They don't bother me at all. Except when they barge into Jeanie's apartment at midnight."

Jeanie frowned, pulling the manila envelope from her pocketbook. "Here. This is what I wanted to show you." She handed Market the first letter. He took it, but continued talking to Paul. "You mean they're bothering her to come back?"

"You better let Jeanie tell you."

Market glanced down at the letter, then began to read with interest, reaching for one after another as Jeanie handed them to him.

Jeanie sat on the edge of her chair, staring at the lively expressions that passed over Market's face as he read, feeling her excitement mount and rear back as she handed him the final photocopy. There. It was done. She had chosen a side, though the choice was a thousand times more difficult and complicated each time than she had imagined when she was young.

Market spread the letters out on his desk, glancing from one to the other. "This is fascinating," he said. "I suspected this, but it's the first solid evidence I've had. Do you have the originals?"

"Yes, of the letters. I only have a photocopy of the check though because . . . they cashed it."

Market nodded without looking up. "I have to see the originals before I go public with this." He looked up, smiling. "I'm not doubting your honesty, Ms. Burger, but it is possible to falsify photostats and I try to be overcareful. Do you think you can get the originals to me today?"

"Uh," Jeanie glanced at Paul. "It will take some hustling.

They're in a bank which closes at three. I guess it's possible."

Market read the letters again, and again complimented Jeanie for coming forward. "Your husband is still there, right? The Dennis Blastrom referred to in this letter?"

"We're separated."

Market asked whether she and Dennis had joined All together, how she had stolen the letters, why she had grown disillusioned. She answered in hedging terms, anxious to avoid the pain of too much revelation. So she was surprised when he asked if she wanted to appear on his show tonight. She said she thought it was important for people to know that the federal government was supporting All and that she'd go on his show to say it.

"Yeah, but why?" Paul blurted out. "Why should Congress give them money?"

Market smiled with his mustache. "The next logical question."

Jeanie glanced quickly at Paul, who looked more attentive than he had all day. She wasn't sure what to answer. It was with just that question in mind that she had clung to the coalition when she returned to New York. What would Gail say to that?

Market held up the one letter that had always puzzled Jeanie. "The Directorate of Science and Technology, this is what interests me most. Did you ever hear of them? They're not part of HEW. They don't give out 'drug rehabilitation funds.'" Market began to read the letter:

Dear Mr. Cordite:

Welcome aboard Joe! Sorry it took so long but we had to override the OMB and appeal directly to the chief. Your group has been awarded the contract. You will keep the same contacting agent, who will work closely with you and advise on internal security. The division is looking forward to new advances in tradecraft! Good luck.

Yours,
Harvey Jones

Market stood up, pacing behind his desk on his Western heels. "Contract, not grant. I wonder if Zinger really is getting HEW money or if they're just putting their names on the checks."

"That sounds like the CIA to me," Paul said. " 'Welcome aboard!' Who would write that, except the Navy?"

Market nodded. "It must be. The CIA has a secret budget. They funnel money through other government agencies to pay their bills and set up pensions for employees, just to disguise where it's coming from."

Jeanie felt chilled. As if the men with black shiny shoes were waiting for her in the lobby. She didn't want Leelannee to see those shoes. "I think we're getting carried away. I know Zinger is playing around with some drug rehabilitation money, but he's not in the CIA. He's not a spy. It doesn't make sense."

"It's not a matter of spying." Market held the letter up to the gray light from the window. "God, I'm dying to see the original of this. Science and Technology is a division of the CIA. It's a research branch." He tapped the letter with his finger. "Advances in tradecraft. What kind of research could they be doing in the Church of All?"

Jeanie stood up too, walking back and forth in front of his desk. "Dennis Blastrom is always doing some kind of research. That's why they call him Brainstorm. I don't know what he's doing."

"How can you not know?" Paul asked softly.

"It got me upset. We didn't discuss it."

"Why did it get you upset?" Paul tapped her leg with his shoe and she turned to look at him.

"He was just trying to create the perfect high. He thought he was some kind of an alchemist who could turn home-grown marijuana into Acapulco Gold."

Market laughed. "I can't imagine the CIA would be interested in that, but who knows? Ms. Burger, you've been great. I don't want to keep you too long. If you can get those originals for me and be back here, say, two hours before show time, we can have one terrific story tonight."

He walked them to the door, shaking hands with Paul, holding on to Jeanie's for an extra moment. "By the way, did you know Helena Carpenter?"

Jeanie shook her head. "She was after my time. But there were other heiresses wandering around when I was there. Cordite would bring in these kids Faye had gone to private school with, and Eli would convert them."

"See if you can remember some of their names," Market said. "We'll talk about it later."

Jeanie's legs felt numb as she left the office. The bank was all the way uptown. She wanted it to be over but it just went on and on. And it wasn't a clean fight. As much as she recoiled from All she didn't hate the people in it. It wasn't their fault if All had become a government arm. It couldn't be the fault of Eli Zinger, gifted with a power of leadership almost beyond his control. Nor even of Dennis Blastrom whose brilliance soared forward without the heavy weight of ethics.

When they reached the elevator Paul put his arm around her. "Well, Jeanie, you sure are an interesting girl." She leaned on him, stilling her thoughts, letting him stroke her head. "I mean none of my other bodyguarding assignments have ever been so exciting, and dangerous."

"You think this is dangerous?" she murmured.

"Dangerous? No. The people who work for the CIA are really Boy Scouts at heart. They wouldn't hurt a fly."

"Oh, Market's off the wall with the CIA thing."

He twisted her curls around his fingers, smiling into her deep eyes. "Let's hope so."

"Yeah, let's hope so." She felt for the small roll of fat above his belt and pinched him. "How was I? Did I sound like something to contend with?"

"I think I liked you better when you were throwing rocks at the mayor's office."

"Do we have time to eat?" Jeanie asked as they skirted around another group of tourists in the lobby. "Maybe I better call my parents first. What do you think I should wear on television?"

Paul shrugged. "You'll have to ask your mother that one."

11

Jeanie left Paul at the coffee shop and went to the phone booth. She called her father at his shop, shouting to make herself heard over the roar of the printing machines. She asked him to meet her to get the documents out of his safe deposit box. He balked, reluctant to leave the shop at midday, forcing her to explain why she needed them. "It's no good, taking that risk, Jean. It won't do any good. Nothing seems to do any good today." She listened patiently to his objections, then repeated the place and time she would meet him. "At least call your mother and see what she has to say," he added, but Jeanie could hear that he was ready to take off his apron, scrub the ink from his fingers, and do as she asked him.

She hung up and dialed Gail's number. Gail was the only person she didn't have to hedge her ideas with. Gail would replate her confidence, which had been rubbed black in spots by her father, by the fancy office building, even by Paul's casualness. The phone rang ten times. Jeanie hung up and dialed the loft. The line was busy. She sighed and went out of the booth to collect Paul.

She found him talking to Justino and Gail. The three of them leaned against the gilded edges of the CRA Building in their blue nylon ski jackets. Jeanie glanced around, wondering where Leelannee was.

Gail put her arm around Jeanie before she could ask any questions. She led her outside to sit on a stone step. "Something really bad has happened," she said quickly. "Your husband came to my house with one of his goons. He took Leelannee."

The skyscrapers that surrounded them seemed to tilt and stagger forward. Gail held on to Jeanie's shoulder tightly, forcing her to look down from the buildings, into her face. "Oh Jeanie, I tried to stop them. He was with this big bald guy who was holding me, and I used my karate kick on him and he finally buckled right over, but by that time Dennis had her in the car. . . ."

"Was it a green Chrysler?"

"No. A little blue car. I went to the police right away. They said they couldn't do a thing. It technically isn't a kidnapping."

Jeanie ground her palms against the stone step. It was very cold. "I don't have a custody agreement. I was afraid to let them know where I was living, so I never started the divorce."

"Oh damn it, Jeanie, I'm sorry. I never imagined this could happen." Gail's arms moved clumsily around her body. Her face looked swollen. "I feel so terrible. Here you were doing the hard thing in there talking to Market and all I had to do was look after . . . and I . . ."

"It's not your fault," Jeanie said flatly. She should have warned Gail. She should have known they could be dangerous. What was the matter with her that she didn't figure that out? She yearned to have her arms around her daughter, to stroke her apple-smooth cheeks. Justino and Paul walked up to them. Paul put a dozen questions to Gail, who became angrier each time she described the scene. They talked to Jeanie, but she couldn't answer because she had no voice, only feelings. She was trembling with anger at herself. Marching boldly into battle regardless of the risks. Exposing Eli, was she? or just exposing the child to danger? She shuddered to think of Leelannee with Dennis, open to the shining faces of those who thought they were gods.

It was possible to simply capitulate. Give up. You win. I lose. Sorry, Eddie Market, I can't get those originals because the documents are forged. I just made up the whole thing to get attention. Would that bring the child back? Perhaps. The gray skyscrapers seemed to take another step toward her, closing the open circle of the plaza.

"We're going to help you get her back," Gail said. "We're just gonna have to take her. The whole coalition will help." She turned to Justino for confirmation. He nodded slowly. "Whatever we can do, we do."

Jeanie took Paul's outstretched arm and stood up. Against the egg-colored sky the buildings leaped back in startling 3-D, like the pop-out pages of a children's book.

"What are you going to do?" Paul asked. His eyes drew her in, like fast moving waters, but she could see he felt inadequate to her pain.

"Do you have any dimes?" She lay the row of dimes on the shelf of the outside phone booth. One by one she used them up, exchanging them for outraged sympathy from her father, advice from her father's lawyer. She didn't dare call her mother. As she spoke she gazed through the thick plastic that surrounded the booth. Paul, Gail, and Justino huddled with their heads bent together like pigeons pecking at crumbs. Then Paul moved toward her through the crowd of swift-walking men with briefcases, past a lady with kid gloves and an umbrella who glanced at him and smiled with her lipstick. He leaned against the phone booth, trying to get the gist of Jeanie's conversations. She spoke to Eddie Market, brushing off his sympathy, trying to formulate a plan, and then abruptly gave up and said she'd call him later.

Paul gathered her in his arms before she could make another call, leading her to the spot where Gail and Justino waited for them, stalled in the cold amid the stream of people who walked as if they knew where they were going. "Come on, you have to talk this out slowly and carefully. No one's going to come up with any magic solution for you."

Her eyes burned from imaginary smoke. She had to pull something good out of the ashes. It's easy to betray yourself for the sake of your children, she thought. Her parents had done it. At least it had seemed that way to her at the time. They'd dropped out of politics to protect their children. They'd moved to the safety of Avocado Towers and she saw them collapse from heroic fighters to smaller-than-life figures. When her parents had sacrificed principle for safety she'd felt herself dissolving as a person. She'd vowed never to copy them.

Everything and everyone was moving that year. She was in junior high. She was old enough to know better. She was old enough not to ask too many questions, but to register their betrayals in disgusted silence. Aunt Claire and Uncle Leon were moving to Connecticut where Leon had gotten his first management-level job. "Leon will make a great boss!"

Father laughed in triumph. But a year later Jay himself was opening his own small print shop, and earning over the income limits for city housing. Mother was glad and sad about leaving the projects. "Glad because it'll take the FBI at least a year to find us again," she laughed as she tossed the scratched plastic dishes in the garbage and wrapped newspaper around the glasses. "And sad because we're moving out of an integrated neighborhood, away from the Tenant's League, and all our friends."

The solid squares of pavement beneath Jeanie's life were cracking up. It was like a rainy day when long worms wiggled up between the squares. She swore she wouldn't let her soul be moved. She'd still be standing under the tree when it began to fruit.

"Stop mooning and wrap up those dishes," Mother said. "Evan, bring me another carton."

She stared at her mother. "Avocado Towers. Of all places!"

"Yes, it's not my idea of perfection either," her mother said, wiping her forehead and leaving a streak of dust across it. "But it'll be good for you kids."

It chilled Jeanie to think they were moving for *her* sake, that they wanted her to be one of the teenagers in coordinated clothes who went out with boys in sports cars. That's not who she was.

The first morning at Avocado Towers they were all in the elevator heading for work and school. It was crowded. Full of women in plastic rain hats and men with large black umbrellas. The elevator stopped on every floor to pick up more couples in hot raincoats and tight shriveled expressions on their faces. In the lobby they moved to the plate-glass window to stare at the pounding rain. The crowd shuddered in one motion, like an giant amoeba, as they watched the rain, tightened the plastic around their heads, and unsnapped the little loops on their umbrellas.

"We're all crazy," Father said suddenly. "This country would fall apart if not for the craziness of the middle class. The damn work ethic."

People nodded. "I haven't missed a day at the office in two years," a woman said. "That should certify me as insane."

Father held the door for her. "You can't help it," he joked. "The place would fall apart without you."

Sheets of gray water smashed against the sidewalk. Jeanie felt the corners of her heart were chewed and bleeding. "So now we're part of the middle class, are we?" she asked. "I thought it was the working class that kept this country going?"

He had to pump the pedal several times to get the car started. "Everyone in America is middle class, Jeanie. Haven't you heard?"

She had despised her parents for protecting her. Perhaps she should have been grateful. The FBI had lost interest in them. The park near Avocado Towers was safe. Was she giving Leelannee that? She tried to regain her sense of power. The other side always makes moves you don't expect. It's because they're bastards. You're not to blame.

"What are you up to?" Gail asked. They gathered around Jeanie, trying quietly to lead her out of herself into the here and now.

"I called Market, my parents, the lawyer."

"And?"

"Now I can call Faye Zinger."

"Okay, good," Paul said. "What are you going to say?"

The palms of Jeanie's hands were tingling with desire to touch her child. "I'll ask them how Leelannee is. I'll ask to speak to her."

"Do you think she's with this Faye?" Gail asked, tapping

her fists against her thighs, her body tensed and leaning forward as if she was waiting for a gunshot to start a race.

"I guess they've got her at the Reverence Hotel. That's their New York headquarters. Don't you listen to the news?"

"You have Faye's phone number?"

"Yeah, she gave it to me."

Justino, who had been quiet all this time, spoke softly. "Tell her you are not alone, that the coalition is behind you, the news media is behind you, that you have lawyers and a group of concerned politicians. Don't sound weak."

Jeanie could barely breathe as she heard Faye's phone ringing. Faye answered it herself, in a gay voice. "The Church of All, you've called the right place."

"This is Jeanette."

"Oh yes, Jeanette."

"How's Leelannee?" She thought if she used as few words as possible her voice wouldn't crack or choke.

"Oh, she's fine, she's playing in the nursery with the other children."

"I'd like to talk to her," Jeanie said.

"Of course, come right up, any time. We're always expecting you."

"Yes, I'll come, but I intend to leave with Leelannee. My lawyers and many people—"

"Oh, lawyers, you don't need lawyers. You have a right to see her, she's your child. It's natural law. I'll see you later and we'll talk. God be with you."

Jeanie stood for a moment with the dead phone to her ear, then hung up. She walked slowly from the phone booth back to the bench where the others were conferring anxiously. It seemed like the hundredth time she'd made the journey in the bitter wind. But as she told them about her conversation she began to feel better. Faye seemed willing to negotiate. It wasn't that they expected to try to keep the child. It wasn't that Dennis Blastrom had suddenly had his fatherly instincts aroused. It must simply be a matter of the documents. She shed the burdened feeling that hung on her limbs. She shook her parents' leaps and retreats out of her head. Even her dread of seeing Brainstorm was set aside.

"I have to go to the Reverence to get Leelannee," she told them. "I'll make the best bargain I can, that's all."

"You're not going in there by yourself," Paul insisted. "I saw those people last night. They looked like they'd do anything they felt like."

Jeanie touched his shoulder, then leaned toward him. "I'd love to have you go with me. But I don't think they'll allow it. Even in Vancouver Eli Zinger was very strict about visitors."

They began to walk down toward the parking lot. "You can't go alone," Paul repeated.

"Maybe some telephone repairmen . . . repairpeople . . . will visit you there," Justino said.

"Yeah," Gail nodded, "maybe some people from Con Edison, or delivering herbal teas, or something."

Paul glanced at Gail and Justino. "She can't go alone."

Gail nodded. "No, she won't be alone."

12

The old hotel had been abandoned for several years before the Church of All purchased it and christened it the Reverence. Paul pulled up under the broad cement canopy, turned off the motor, and gave Justino the car keys. "Don't smash it up, my insurance is already high."

"I'll drive," Gail said. "Let me have the registration."

"You better wait here a few minutes," Jeanie said, "to see whether they let Paul come in."

They went over, one more time, the contingency plans they'd worked out on the short ride downtown. Jeanie was carefully examining the building before stepping out. The hotel had a long rectangular base with a tower of flesh-colored brick standing on top of the lower building. The tower windows were supported by winged gargoyles. It was a beautiful structure, elegant in its attempt to soar above the common street life of Tenth Avenue.

Jeanie's senses were burning with alertness. She leaned over and hugged Paul tightly. They got out of the car, nodding to Gail and Justino. The bitter wind hit her as she hurried toward the revolving entrance. Paul was a step behind her with his hand on her shoulder. She peered through the glass door as if she expected to see Leelannee playing on the lobby floor.

There was no wind inside, but the unheated area was cold. The girls at the reception desk looked up and their smiles seemed to flash on simultaneously. The lobby was flanked by staircases that were closed off by tall iron gates. In front of them was a glass door with a banner over it which proclaimed: URBAN CRUSADE—A SONG OF CITIES.

Jeanie's heart beat as if she had run a long way. It was Paul who led her to the man sitting in a wooden chair near a wall phone. He was the bald, older man who had come to Jeanie's apartment. She noticed the needlepoint canvas on his lap and reached out to touch the stitches. He pulled the canvas away and stood up, his face twitching in a struggle to control his emotion. Unconsciously his arm cradled his stomach and Jeanie thought with satisfaction that this must be the stomach that Gail had kicked.

Jeanie jerked her hand toward the needlepoint. "It's very nice."

He grunted, rolled up the canvas, and pushed it into his jacket pocket. He picked up the wall phone and said, "Jeanette Burger has arrived." Then, "She's got her friend with her. Certainly, as you wish."

Taking a ring of keys out of his pocket, he motioned Jeanie to follow him. His clothes slumped on his frame, like that of a bulky athlete who had lost weight in a sudden illness.

"Thomas, isn't it?" Paul said, attempting to shake his hand. "I met you last night, remember? How's the Chrysler holding up?"

Thomas turned a large key in the iron and glass door, opened it, and went inside. He waited until Jeanie had stepped into the inner lobby to tell Paul that he would have to wait outside.

"He has to come with me," Jeanie said hastily. "He has all the important papers."

"He can't be admitted."

"Look, you took her child. Don't tell me what I have to do. I'm going in." Paul grabbed at Thomas's shoulder, but was shaken off, and the door almost closed on his fingers.

Jeanie gazed at the inner lobby, feeling a draft on all sides without Paul's protective warmth. The room looked like the floor of a convention, with scattered literature tables, film booths, and hundreds of people wearing bright gold discs on their shirts and beaming smiles on their faces. The noise level was low. Thomas gave her a strained smile. "I'm sorry I had to exclude your friend. We have a policy about—"

"I know, I know," she snapped, still trying to take in the huge room. The ceiling was made of iron diamonds filled with glass. There were huge chandeliers giving a rosy light. It was a beautiful old building. She might have advised Eli to buy it herself if she were still his advisor. In a building like this the roof would probably be strong enough to support a garden.

She followed Thomas across the lobby, gazing in wonderment at everything. It was like coming home and finding your parents had struck it rich and moved to a mansion. In 1969 they'd pooled their dollars to buy the land in Vancouver, and now All owned this expensive piece of New York real estate.

As she passed Allees leading new converts through the exhibits she became hypnotized by the gold discs that flashed by her. She recognized faces as they passed but the names didn't come to her at once and she didn't stop anyone. They seemed to be marching, though not in military posture; there was a measured sense to their movements as if they were all walking to the same inner rhythm.

Thomas brought her to a central booth and called for Helena Carpenter, who popped up behind the desk with a wobbly, birdlike movement to her head. White hair seemed to form a tuft on the top of her head and Jeanie thought she looked like a tufted titmouse she had once seen perched on a branch.

"God be with you, Thomas."

Thomas nodded. "You're directed to take Ms. Burger up to see Faye."

The girl cocked her head to the side. "Are you coming with us, Thomas?"

"No."

"Why not? Come for a ride in the elevator."

He shook his head in annoyance and his face grew purple. It seemed to Jeanie he spent a lot of energy suppressing his emotions. In a few seconds he regained his impassive expression. "I have to report now."

"Thomas, Eli explained that taking elevator rides with

friends is very restful. Especially going up to the tower. The huuuuuum of the motor . . ."

Thomas turned on his heel and walked away. Helena giggled. "He's so sensitive." She turned to Jeanie, spreading her hands palms up, fingers splayed. "I'll take you to the tower to see her godship."

She tried to walk a bit ahead of Jeanie as they crossed toward the elevators, but Jeanie took big steps to keep up with her. She was eager to make some contact to break the murmuring voices of the followers streaming past them. "Miss Carpenter, how do you like it here?"

Helena turned her blue swimming pool eyes on Jeanie. "Oh, I love it here. We all do. Eli Zinger explains everything. You must be so glad to return." She stretched her arms out awkwardly.

Glad to return. So Helena knew who she was, who she had been. Was it a matter of public discussion in the Church? "Don't you miss life with your parents?" Jeanie asked. Helena looked no more than eighteen.

"Oh no. My parents . . . they always made such a fuss about my learning to read. Eli explains that if your heart is with God you don't have to read." Two red spots appeared on her almost albino skin. She craned her neck to watch Thomas heading for another elevator.

"Well, parents worry," Jeanie said. "Maybe you saw *my* daughter today. I think she came in with Thomas and Dennis Blastrom. She's about this high . . . four years old . . . talks a mile a minute."

"I was out spreading the word all day," Helena said. "It was wonderful."

The elevator arrived and they stepped inside. "Well, if you do see my daughter . . ." Jeanie began, but Helena seemed to go off in a trance, with a smile on her face as if she were remembering something very pleasurable. Probably the meditation room, Jeanie thought. She touched Helena's bony arm. "Her name's Leelannee . . . if you do see her, would you tell her her mother's here?" She tried to get a yes or no from Helena but the girl was experiencing the upward motion of the elevator and didn't move until it stopped on the top, the twenty-first floor.

"This way, her godship's waiting for you."

The faded, stained red carpet that covered the rest of the hotel had been replaced on the twenty-first floor. The carpet was deep blue and so thick it was difficult to walk on. The paint on the walls looked new too, white with baroque gold trim. There was a mirrored table holding a tall vase of white roses. Helena walked in front of her now, past door after door on which the old hotel numbers had been carefully removed and painted over. It seemed fitting to be escorted through this luxury by a girl who had so recently owned a half million dollars. She's heiress of the month, Jeanie thought, trying to recall the names of other heiresses who enjoyed special attention until Eli forgot them.

Helena knocked on the door, then pushed it open to let Jeanie in. Faye Zinger was reclining on a lounge near the window of a large room. She smiled, waving slightly to Jeanie, carefully placing a leather bookmark in the thin volume of *Explanations by Eli Zinger* that she was reading. The lines on Faye's forehead seemed less dark and deep today. Her long hair was brushed over the shoulders of her pale-rose gown. "Would you please close the door, Jeanette? Helena has difficulties remembering our ways."

Jeanie closed the door and sat down on a tapestry chair near Faye. "You look good today, Faye."

"Oh, thank you. My whole system has improved since I eliminated pepper from my diet." She motioned to the concave eye mirror on her nightstand. "The pool of Diana under my right pupil has also dissolved. I don't know why I was still using pepper. Eli explained the damage it causes years ago."

Jeanie touched the fur stole that was draped across Faye's lap. It must be ermine. Incredible. Ermine and rose-gold rooms for the Queen to swoon on in her cloud-covered tower. Jeanie could still remember the dirt streaks on the toes sticking out of Faye's sandals the first time they met on Sixth Avenue. She glanced at the large TV screeen against the wall which showed a picture of the lobby where Allees were leading new converts on journeys of self-discovery.

"I've got to hand it to you, Faye. You made it. And you have it made. This fur is real, right?"

"It was a gift from the followers. Eli explained that it is our duty to accept love in whatever form it arrives."

"Well, I'm impressed. And I guess impressing people is your business."

"It's not a business. The Church of All is a project for spiritual and social change." She said the words slowly, as if she were expecting Jeanie to memorize them.

Jeanie smiled. "I love the change that's come over little Helena Carpenter. Isn't she the one who was always in the news—the dumb little heiress jetting around the globe with Iranian playboys? It's wonderful how Eli's managed to salvage her, spiritually and socially I mean."

Faye sniffed and her eyes, which were faceted like a piece of coal, seemed to tear.

"Oh shit," Jeanie said, "I'm sorry. I should have known she was Eli's latest."

Faye took a deep breath. "Some souls are given to us to care for." Her voice dropped. "I haven't had a confidante since you left, Jeanette. It's not fair to provoke me now. I can't very well—"

"Fair? When my daughter is sitting on my lap we'll talk

about fair!" Jeanie's anger began to dim all the glamour of the room.

"Jeanette, you are thwarting us for no reason. You must re-enter now, for the sake of your soul. Then you would have no troubles with Leelannee. You belong here. This is your place and it's a place of honor." Faye's eyes were glowing. "We were sisters together. Sisters and friends bound in a sigh of transcendence. Your despair shines from you like a light in a tower."

Jeanie scratched her fingernails along the brocaded arm of her chair. "I'm anxious about Leelannee."

"Would you like to see her? There's nothing to worry about. We nurture our young." Faye picked up a remote control device and changed the channel on the television screen. It flashed to the blue carpeted hallway where Helena was leaning over a desk looking as if she were telling secrets to Thomas Baker. Faye smiled, then flashed by the other channels quickly, from empty room to empty room, until a picture of children filled the screen. A group of preschoolers were exercising with rods about the size of yardsticks. They held them over their heads, mouthing some words, then lowered them to their waists, their knees, the floor. Faye pushed another button and the picture took a long view. Jeanie saw Leelannee sitting in a rocking chair in the corner of the room. She had her thumb in her mouth and her eyes almost crossed as she sucked. A moon-faced woman approached Leelannee and offered her a rod, but the child kicked it away.

Faye flipped the channel back to the scene in the hallway with Thomas and Helena. "Eli should be very interested in this. I think I'll tape it." She leaned over and pushed another button.

"Leelannee looks so unhappy. She's scared and tired. It's really mean to keep her in there with those strange children."

"Oh, it's so good for her," Faye said earnestly. "The years

before the change of teeth are the time to help a child develop natural powers. The biospiritual clock . . ."

"I don't want her learning that crap." Jeanie was on her feet leaning over Faye. "I want her to learn how to cross the street and read and stick up for herself. . . ."

The door opened loudly and Mr. Cordite, Faye's father and the business manager of the Church of All, stepped heavily into the room. Jeanie had the distinct feeling he had been watching them on the closed-circuit TV just as Faye watched Thomas and Helena in the hall. "Sit down, Jeanette," he said sharply, closing the door with a bang. He glanced at the image on the TV screen of Helena begging Thomas to let her touch his needlepoint. "Would you turn that off?" Faye pushed the button and the screen turned brown. "Now let's talk truth, Ms. Burger."

Faye moved her feet and he sat next to her on the lounge, leaning toward Jeanie, his thick hands resting on his knee, the gold disc on his shirt glaring in her eyes. "Did you or did you not join All of your own free will?"

"What's that supposed to mean?"

"You're not accusing us of kidnapping you or brainwashing you, or some other hogwash?"

"I'm not accusing you of anything. I want to see my daughter and take her home. That's all."

Cordite rubbed his palms on his pants and stroked his thin gray hair. "When you joined All you signed a lifetime contract. Your earnings became the property of the Church of All. Your possessions were turned over. Your offspring became—"

"That's ridiculous," Jeanie said. "It wasn't even the Church of All when I joined. It was a socialist commune in Vancouver. And I was always free to leave. No judge would agree that Leelannee is your property." She was sharpened to the conflict. It was better than Faye's edgy politeness. It was clear from Cordite's deep-red face that he would like to break both her legs.

"Judges? Yes, they rule where they have jurisdiction. Eli Zinger is the judge here. You left without permission. Now that you've come back voluntarily, I'm sure that will count in your favor."

They stared at each other for a moment, Jeanie still not realizing what his message was. "What do you want from me?"

Faye crossed the room to an inlaid marble desk and took a sheet out of the drawer. She handed Jeanie a golden pen. "Sign the request for re-entrance. Eli will explain further. In his presence all things are clarified."

"Faye, you know I came here to get Leelannee. I don't want to re-enter."

Cordite stared at his shoes. Faye stroked her face delicately with her long fingers. "I know that part of you longs to re-enter. You want to be with your child."

What was she saying? Jeanie was at a loss to decipher the subtleties because her heart was pounding so loudly.

Cordite stood up, hitching up his pants over his large bottom, the coins jingling loudly in his pocket. "If you want to be with your child, you better sign."

"A lot of people," Jeanie said slowly, "know that I didn't come up here to re-enter. Media people, a group of concerned politicians, my parents. You aren't going to be able to fool them."

"We'll worry about relating to the outside world," Cordite said. "If you want to see your daughter . . ."

"What do you want me for at this point?" Jeanie asked. "You don't need reluctant converts. If it's those letters that are bothering you . . ." She hated to admit having stolen the letters. She could hear Market's delight at having his first concrete evidence. But she hoped that this retreat was only strategic; that it would put her in a better position to attack later.

"We're not interested in the letters," Cordite said.

"That's the truth," Faye agreed. "You must sign. Don't thwart us, Jeanette. The pulsing of the lodestar is irresistible."

She stood up, feeling ready to leave, hoping that Justino had managed to get the floor plans of the Reverence Hotel and would help break into the nursery to get her child. "I'm sure the court will give me custody of Leelannee."

"Dennis and his daughter are leaving for Vancouver in under an hour," Cordite said. "Unless there's some change of plans."

Jeanie knew it was true from the way Faye turned her eyes away while Cordite studied her head on. She would have to sign. It was only a piece of paper. If they took Leelannee to the Vancouver farm she'd never see her again. What kind of tactics were these? She remembered how absurd she thought Market was when he mentioned the CIA. But what the hell did she know about the CIA? A pair of black polished shoes across a lobby floor. A hasty move to Avocado Towers. "If I sign"—Faye looked up, smiling—"will I have free access to Leelannee? She won't have to stay in the nursery all the time?"

"Things will return to normal," Faye said. "When you need each other's influence, you'll be together. When you need time apart, she will be in the nursery. The mother and father work it out."

"You actually expect me to go back to Dennis?"

"It's not necessary," Cordite said. "We have divorces here."

Faye touched her shoulders, pulling her back in the chair, massaging briefly to relax her. "Soon you will feel so relieved. Worldly entanglements will be far behind you. There was no reason to leave the Church because you and Dennis were having difficulties. Our planets can change positions and still revolve around the sun."

"Let me see Leelannee now."

Faye pushed the remote-control button, but Leelannee must have been out of camera range because she kept picking up other young faces. Faye handed her the pen. "Sign, your godship. Then you can go down to the nursery and find the relief you long for. Every woman loses power if she's out of her child's influence too long."

As soon as she had signed Cordite took the paper. He looked triumphant. He kissed his daughter on the forehead as he left, then called from the doorway. "Do you want me to tell Eli or do you think you'll be seeing him in the next two or three days?"

"I'll carry the message," Faye said. She shook her head, smiling at Jeanette. "Mr. Cordite still has some rusty views. He takes it as a personal insult that Eli isn't hanging around to service my every need. The man has thousands of souls depending on him. . . ."

"I guess Eli is plenty dependent on your father."

"No. Why do you say that?" Faye opened a sliding closet which revealed a row of gowns.

"Well, for the money and for the connections in high places."

"Jeanette. Your head is filled with worldly nonsense. You're going to feel so differently in a few hours, I don't even want to argue with you. When you see Eli you'll understand." She opened a box and took out a gold disc pin. "Put this on so you don't alarm security." Jeanie pinned the gold disc to her shirt. Faye talked aimlessly about spheres and orbits. Jeanie managed to make out that she was busy preparing for tomorrow night's rally and that she saw herself as progressing to a higher level each day.

Jeanie studied the corners of the room near the ceiling.

She couldn't find any television eyes. Perhaps Faye's room was not watched, though Cordite's entrance had been timed too perfectly for her to believe that. The presence of television cameras seemed a logical extension of the policy of "watching out for each other" she had grown used to on Vancouver. It had amounted to a constant scrutiny of each other's words, actions, gestures to guard against lingering willfulness and selfishness.

"Are you ready for tea now?" Faye asked. "Or lunch? The food in the leadership dining room is much better here than in Vancouver."

"I'm not hungry," Jeanie said. "I just want to see Leelannee."

"Oh, of course. I'll call Helena, if you don't mind. She's on escort service now."

Jeanie noticed that she didn't use the telephone on the desk but a pocket microphone to call the hall security desk. They had a hell of a lot of equipment. It was amazing. She remembered the day they had a big debate over whether to farm with tractors or hand tools. Jeanie had urged machine farming, partly out of fear of starving and partly from the conviction that the trend toward primitivism at the All commune was foolish. But she had never imagined that tractors could lead to electronic surveillance—designed to protect them from intruders, of course.

Jeanie glanced at herself in Faye's long mirror. She tried to take the hard alertness from her features, to smile with sincerity and sunshine. She didn't want to be stared at in the drafty hall. For the time being she needed to walk and think in step.

13

When the knock came on the door it was Thomas Baker, not Helena, who waited for Jeanette. Faye looked slightly surprised. "I called for Helena. I just needed her to show Jeanette where the nursery is."

"Mr. Cordite sent me," Thomas said.

He walked down the corridor next to Jeanie, his shoulder bumping against her occasionally. Jeanie missed Paul. She missed the freedom to turn left or right at any corner. But she didn't feel uncomfortable. It felt somehow natural to be back in the fold, as if the hassles of her workaday life in the Bronx were just a temporary aberration from the years of directed peace. It was a struggle to remain observant. She tried to keep her eyes in motion so she wouldn't grow numb. Vases filled with white roses. Clean paint in the halls. A carpet so blue her feet drowned in it. The elevator was not smooth. It had a stool for an operator and elaborate brass fixtures, even though a modern push-button system had been installed. Thomas rang four.

Twenty-one was Faye. Four was the nursery. Jeanie wondered if she'd be staying the night and where they'd put her. She wondered without alarm and had to force bolts of anxiety to keep herself alert. She was accepting too easily. It reminded her of her parents' reaction when she and Dennis first entered All. Her father said utopian socialism was a wild pursuit of fanciful ideas, that Karl Marx had proved that a hundred years ago. But they let them go, and even made cash contributions so the commune could buy a tractor. Her parents' communism had changed into a liberalism so extreme that they accepted anybody's right to do anything. And when she'd returned from New York, without Dennis, without much explanation, they again did little to influence her. Her father made a token remark about the coalition—"Do you kids have to make the exact same mistakes we did? Can't you think of some new mistakes?"—but if Jeanie pressured him he printed up their leaflets for free. She mustn't be so accepting. If Cordite put her in a private room tonight she must insist on the dormitory, say she needed to humble herself. In the dormitory she might find someone who missed the outside enough to help her. Maybe they could make a call for her. Help! I'm trapped in the tower of my own past beliefs.

The fourth floor had not been remodeled. The carpet was thready. The tables in the alcoves were wobbly, or propped against the wall with a leg missing. The paint was streaked with sweaty fingerprints. It smelled like an old hotel. She could hear the nursery before Thomas's broad hand gestured to the right. There were about twenty-five children. The members of All were not a fertile lot. Birth control, though supposedly carried out through the direction of suppressed semen to higher energies, was actually sold on the contraband ring that kept drugs and sugary foods circulating in All. Since money was not used by All members, the contraband was paid for by sexual favors, taking over work assignments, putting in good words to the right people. Eddie Market had taken notes when Jeanie told him that part of her story. He said several newspaper writers had commented on the low birth rate in the Church. But Jeanie thought minor forms of corruption were not too significant.

She had to admit that the children looked quite happy. They were playing quietly, drawing pictures, rocking dolls. She didn't spot Leelannee at first, because her daughter had crawled under a table with another girl and they were whispering in each other's ears.

"There's my mommy!" Leelannee said, bumping her head as she scrambled out from under the table.

And Jeanie had her in her arms, rocking her, stroking her apple cheeks, and smoothing stray hairs out of her eyes. Leelannee's legs dangled against her body. She wanted just to run with her, down the corridor and out into the street, but Thomas's bulky body blocked the doorway. She carried Lee to the far end of the nursery and sat in a chair with her on her lap. While she was wondering what she could say that would guide the child without alarming her, Leelannee began to babble about her adventures.

"You know who came to Gail's house, Mommy? Mommy! You know who? My daddy, Dennis. And Gail went running after the car, Mommy, and she kicked someone. I saw her kick someone. Dennis, Daddy, says Gail is a bad guy. Is she? Is Gail a bad guy, Ma? I thought Gail was a good guy." She was speaking very loudly, and Jeanie glanced at the attendants and children but they didn't appear to notice.

She stroked Leelannee's hair. "Gail is not a bad guy. Dennis is wrong." She tried to keep her voice low without attracting attention by whispering. "I love you very much. Do you love Mommy?"

Leelannee responded by kissing and hugging her neck.

"You remember Paul, right?"

Leelannee nodded.

"Well maybe, just maybe, Gail and Paul will come and get you and take you home sometime. If they do, you're supposed to go with them very quietly."

"I want to go home with you!" Leelannee shouted. Then she caught sight of her friend waiting for her under the table. "Do I have to go home right now? Can't I play a little longer? Daddy's going to take me on an airplane ride."

Jeanette gave up and just held on to the child without talking. There was no sense adding to her confusion. She felt proud of Leelannee's resiliency. Perhaps this child could survive growing up in the Church and come out intact.

When Thomas and the nursery attendants motioned that it was time to go, Leelannee kissed her goodbye and ran back to join her friend under the table.

Jeanie stopped the moon-faced attendant at the doorway. "If she gets upset, please call for me. She's new here. . . ."

"She's an old soul. You don't have to worry."

"Um, tell me, do you give the children any drug preparations?"

"Only if the doctor prescribes it."

Jeanie wondered if Dennis Blastrom was considered the doctor now. "I wanted to tell you that Leelannee is allergic to most medications. It gives her heart palpitations."

"I'm glad you mentioned that. I'll leave a message for the others."

Jeanie left the room, carefully suppressing a smile. She knew that Dennis had sometimes recommended laudanum for babies whose cries interrupted the meditation sessions. Leelannee was not allergic to anything, but perhaps they'd be afraid to take a chance.

The elevator did not go up to the twenty-first floor but back to the lobby. A group of followers got in. They were all young, with thin health-food faces. One turned to Jeanie with a surprised nod. "Welcome back, your godship."

Jeanie nodded. She didn't remember his name.

"May you follow the lodestar without losing your way," the young man said.

Jeanie noticed the television eye at shoulder level in the corner of the elevator. The car stopped several times, each time opening onto red stained carpet, so that Jeanie was grateful by the time they reached the twenty-first floor and she could step into the deep blue. Thomas Baker bumped her shoulder as they got out of the elevator. He led her down the hall in the opposite direction from Faye's room. There was a sense of violence lurching in him. Jeanie hoped he had been ordered to leave her alone. They crossed a narrow, guarded corridor. Every few feet there were tall young boys with expressions of peaceful meditation on their faces. Their arms were crossed over their chests. They were in what Jeanie guessed was Eli Zinger's part of the tower. In Vancouver he had his own quadrant, separated from Faye's by acres. Eli's relationship with his wife was a subject of constant speculation among the followers. There were those who sympathized with Faye and rejoiced at the infrequent times they were seen together and Faye glowed from the attention. There were others, mostly the young women, who blamed Faye and her father for the quality of the food, the long work hours, the endless restrictions; they felt that Eli's perfect sense of justice was misinterpreted by Cordite who made all the regulations. Jeanie's high leadership position had been based on her ability to get along with both the Queen and King. She had sympathized with Faye, but hated Cordite, which was an attitude Eli had found especially useful.

Thomas pushed a chair against the wall for Jeanie and sat down himself about two feet away. Across the hall there was a white telephone on a marble table. Jeanie noticed it had no dial and no numbers. It was a house phone. Every phone she had passed in the corridors had been a house phone. Members of the Church of All did not call outside. Jeanie looked for TV cameras but couldn't find any. Perhaps there was wiring under the thick blue carpet. The electronic innovations held her attention: as if it were wires that held the guards in their poses of peaceful attention; as if the followers had been given shock treatments to rid them of all natural anxiety. She thought that Zinger was relying more and more on forgetfulness and isolation to bind his followers. The first year at Vancouver they had all been so free; they had encouraged parents to visit, hoping to convert them too. But then

Eli explained they must shave away all distractions, they must rely on each other and deny the outside world, which could only be salvaged by a universal contagion of peace and harmony. Perhaps the contagion could be speeded up by electronics.

She was too concerned with equipment, she knew that. It wasn't the primary problem. Should she strike a pose? Should she pretend to Eli Zinger that she was back under his charms? He wasn't stupid. He wasn't as naïve as she. Perhaps half a lie was best. I would like to try re-entry for a few days and see how it goes. See how Leelannee adjusts. See if I can stand being around my ex-husband. See if you and I can reach a new understanding, Eli.

The window at the end of the corridor had a blue and green stained glass over the top. It made interesting light patterns on the rug. They were waiting a long time. Thomas Baker had taken out his needlepoint and was weaving the white background threads around the baby deer. He was about two-thirds done with the canvas. When he saw Jeanie watching, he tilted his heavy hands so that she couldn't see the canvas.

"Who are you making that for?" she asked. "A niece or a grandchild or someone?"

He didn't answer, he just wove.

"You can talk to me. I won't corrupt you. I used to do needlepoint myself when I was in All. Otherwise you go crazy." She studied his fleshy face. "Is that a kit? I always hated kits because you run out of thread just when you're two rows from finishing."

He looked up at her. "That happened to me last time!"

"What'd you do?"

"Her godship Faye got me some more brown thread. It wasn't exactly the right shade, but only I can see it."

Jeanie nodded. Now that she had gotten him to talk to her she didn't have anything to say to him. "Will we have to wait a long time?"

Thomas shrugged. He tilted his canvas again and held it close to his face. Jeanie studied his pockets, his waist, his pant legs, to see if she could detect any weapons bulging. Nothing. There was a sign that said FIRE EXIT. Even the Church of All had to comply with some laws. She was tired of sitting in the wooden chair. She stood up and leaned against the wall. Thomas noted her action but did not comment. She poked her toe along the wall, pulling away the rug. There was some sort of wiring under it.

14

The wiring led from a rooftop antenna to the row of television screens in Eli Zinger's studio. Dennis Blastrom—short, thin, curly-haired—was the first to notice the static that broke the TV pictures. He stepped closer to the screens, peering at the broken images. "Look at that," he said. "She's kicking the antenna. I tell you the only thing that's on her mind is getting out of here. Taking Leelannee and leaving."

"We anticipated that." Zinger sat in a tall, carved wood chair with his arms resting on the curved arms. "What I'm concerned about, Dennis, is not your plan but your alarm."

Dennis stared at the screen until Jeanette stopped touching the wire with her foot. "Alarmed? I'm not alarmed. I know we can handle her. In a few hours she will have truly re-entered."

Zinger's voice was deep and low with an edge of rust to

it, like a Jehovah who smoked. "You are alarmed. As much alarmed as Cordite."

"Cordite? I fought Cordite. You heard me. He wanted to pop her off yesterday, before she went to that newsman. I told him—if the Church has to use violent methods, then what does the division need us for? What makes us unique?"

Zinger put his large hands in front of his face. He rocked forward, as if struggling with a great pain. Dennis was at his side immediately. "Your godship. Can I get you something?"

"Yes."

Dennis rummaged in his pocket among the tiny bottles of pills. He gave Zinger two small orange circles. Then he waited a good ten minutes after Zinger had swallowed them for the leader to take his hands away from his tall rectangular face. When he removed his hands Zinger looked serene. His beard and flesh seemed whiter. His calm blue eyes covered the blazing furnace Dennis had glimpsed before. Zinger stood up and examined the painting he had left half finished the day the Church of All was declared. He glanced at Dennis as if he wasn't sure why Dennis was occupying his space. Then he glanced at the television screens which he always kept on to reorient himself when he returned from his inner journeys. "Jeanette has returned. I must greet her."

"We were talking about that," Dennis said. He pushed his round, goggle-shaped glasses back on his nose. "Her re-entry is not voluntary. We're going to have to use a very high quality substance in the meditation room to make her walk in step."

"You want to try the new substance?" His blue eyes were very soft, as if with regret and tenderness. "It's a pity to take chances. . . ."

"I tried it on myself!" Dennis said. "It's a modification of what we used on Alley McDonald, that newspaper reporter who snuck in here to write a story and ended up joining? You remember him?"

Eli spread his hands, palms up. "I have so many."

"Your godship, I hate to bother you with these details, but I think it's important this time. If Jeanette is successfully reintegrated it's going to have a broad effect—way beyond canceling out whatever she said to that newsman, which is all Cordite is worried about. Cordite is going to be forced to write a report to the division saying that the Church of All can now handle resistant types."

Dennis watched carefully for Zinger's reaction. His godship was in a dormant state, with his lizard tongue back in his mouth, with his power concealed. The epilepsy-controlling drug, which Zinger tended to demand after, rather than before, his petit-mal seizures always left him in a subdued state. Dennis was torn between his impatience to try out his new substance and wanting to wait until Zinger recovered his full power.

"You want her back," Zinger shook his head and long beard. "You must kill that desire. She is lost to you. She is not lost to the Church. I want you to accept that before I allow you to direct her meditation."

Dennis ran his hands through his curly hair. His heart bucked in rebellion but he kept still.

"Do you accept that?" Zinger rose from his chair, towering over Dennis. "You are refused permission to mate with Jeanette. I want you to marry someone else, soon."

Dennis nodded slowly. "Of course, as you say, your godhead." He thrilled at using that word, the secretly conferred title which only a few had the right to speak. Yet it felt so appropriate. He had known Eli Zinger for six years, working closely with him every day, yet never growing intimate. It was impossible to be intimate with the godhead.

He had such power, such control. As closely as Dennis watched him Eli Zinger showed no human flaws. Zinger didn't want Jeanette as a bed partner or a friend; he only wanted her inside the protective cloak of the Church of All for her own good.

Zinger's blue gaze held Dennis in a long reflection upon his submission. Then he said: "Prepare the meditation room. I'll see Jeanette now."

"What if she resists going in here?" Dennis asked from the doorway behind the Japanese screen that led to Eli's private meditation room. "I can use lower doses if she's relaxed to begin with."

Eli pressed a buzzer that alerted Thomas outside. "Leave that to me, Dennis." He sat down on a small Oriental mat and faced the green and yellow stained-glass window. He hitched his off-white robe over his knees and slowly placed his legs in full lotus position. His hands rested palms up on his knees, with his thumbs and index fingers forming two circles until he had placed himself deep within his trance, at which point his fingers fell limply from his knees.

Jeanie slowly pushed open the door. The tower was filled with tinted light from the green and yellow stained-glass window. She saw Eli Zinger's back, erect in his white robe, and automatically walked quietly so as not to disturb his trance. The door behind her closed. Her gaze traveled to the bronze Tibetan statues that stood on white pillars and threw contorted shadows on the wall behind them. The room was quiet in the same style as Eli's first corner of privacy in Vancouver. Now the statues were genuinely two thousand years old instead of imitations. Now his paintings were expensively framed instead of hung bare. Now the screen that covered one end of the room was a delicate Japanese painting instead of a cheap Indian bedspread. But unlike Faye, who in a single leap had gone from hippie poverty to nouveau-riche opulence, Eli's tastes had remained steady. Jeanie walked past him to look at the easel at the far end of the room. The half-finished painting made her sad. She remembered the day he had flung away his palette and accepted his leadership role in the newly declared Church of All. It had been a turning point for her as well. She could accept the wildest socialist commune. Bizarre behavior in an artist was easily excused. But a *church*? She could never work up any enthusiasm for religion—even the newest, latest version.

The only chair in the room was Eli's elaborately carved throne. So Jeanie remained standing in front of the easel with the half-finished painting. She had grown so used to waiting that it was a bit of a surprise when Eli, who had come up silently behind her, rested his palm on the top of her reddish hair. "Don't turn yet," he said. There was gaiety in his voice, as if he had his hands over her eyes and was saying Guess who? "You are lost in memories. The memories are sweetening your pain. You are glad to be back, though you will never admit it to anyone, least of all yourself. And right now you are as eager to turn and look at my face as I am to see yours."

He lifted his hand from her head and she turned, smiling, finding great refreshment in his eyes, which were like a panoramic view of blue sky and white clouds. "It's so good to see you again," he said. He touched his fingers to her lips, preventing her from speaking. "There is no one like you, Jeanette. You are unique and perfect. It will take many battles with the system before you become world-weary. You will always have this retreat to return to. And you will always be thinking of leaving. Sometimes I will call you back, as this time. Other times you will come back on your own. Either way is fine." He smiled. His beard and flesh seemed whiter than Jeanie remembered, and his eyes clearer blue. If you had to choose a godhead, he was a logical choice. He could have modeled for Renaissance paintings of saints about to be martyred.

He led her to the small Oriental rug by the window and they sat close together. "Please, Jeanette, speak," he said.

Old habits had seized her mind. She closed her eyes and let her thoughts clear from the sight of him and the room. She saw Leelannee's face. She saw Paul leaning against his car, waiting for her. She opened her eyes and looked at Eli Zinger. "I'm very concerned about Leelannee. I want to take her and I want to go home. My life is not here now. Maybe, as you say, I'll come back sometime. But right now I'm not comfortable here."

Eli nodded. "You haven't tried meditating for a length of time yet. It's a difficult transition from the outside. You know that new initiates meditate for many days. Someone like yourself who achieved such a high level before would not have to go through—"

"I don't want to meditate. I want to spend time with my daughter. It's a very violent shock, you know, having her kidnapped." She stood up suddenly, walking back and forth in front of the window.

Eli got up too, towering over her, standing composed on the green Oriental rug. "The Church of All is not perfect, Jeanette. It made me very sad to approve what happened today. However, it was the most merciful plan presented to me."

"Presented to you! You keep up the illusion that you're really in charge around here, Eli. With all your deep insight you can't see that Cordite and his government friends are using you—"

He held up a finger and she stopped speaking. "We had this conversation before. I told you then, it is I who am using them. You came to me in Vancouver and said the commune was falling apart. You expected me to do something. Without money not a single additional soul would have been liberated."

"Maybe not," Jeanie said, "maybe we should have let the whole thing fall apart." She hadn't brushed her hair in hours and the curls were frizzing around her head. She felt like her head was filled with electricity.

"I have a responsibility, not only to the specific dreams of the founding members, but to all of humanity. Everyone can benefit from what we achieve here. Peace and harmony are contagious."

"Oh, are they?" She was tapping her foot. "Let me ask you this. What do I have to do so that I can take Leelannee and leave?"

He looked suddenly weary and began to walk restlessly along the perimeter of the studio. His step was like a knife on a chopping block. His shadow loomed around the room. He seemed very restless and jerky, then sat down abruptly on his wooden throne and covered his face with his hands.

Jeanie sighed lightly, trying to see the street through the green stained-glass window. She knew she had no choice but to wait out his trance.

It took only a few moments this time. He stood up with clear blue masking the blazing furnace behind his eyes. He put his hands on her shoulders, smiling. "It's fine," he said, in his deepest, mellowest tone, "you can leave with your daughter when you wish."

Elation bounced in Jeanie but she tried to keep it down. "But is it your decision, Eli? What about Cordite?"

"Give Cordite the letters back and you'll go."

"Fine, that's fine, I offered them to him, but he didn't seem interested."

"Leave that to me." He was smiling at her with transcendental light. "It's so good to see the relief in your face." He moved his hands over her face. "We could walk away from here together. Step away from it, go to the mountains and begin again. I believe the same things you believe, Jeanette. I'll follow you this time."

She stepped back, shaking her head. "And the Gods retire to Mount Olympus leaving their followers to burn meat offerings to lure their attention."

"Start over again with the same beliefs," he said, "and see where they lead this time." He leaned over and bent his lips to hers. Warm nibbling flesh amid the hair of beard and mustache. His hands lifted her breasts from below, gently stroking.

She stepped back decisively. "I can't. I'm in love with someone, Eli."

He nodded, unperturbed. "I think it's time to prepare for your leave of absence." He took her arm and led her to the far corner of the room. Behind the Japanese screen was a door she hadn't noticed before. He opened it. "Wait in there for me. It shouldn't take long to arrange things."

She stepped over the high threshold, glad to be out of his overwhelming presence. She was in a small room, a very small room. Three walls were hung with fabric. The door closed behind her with a metallic thud. She could hear him locking it, and each lock made a hissing sound as if a vacuum was being created. She lifted the fabric that covered the door and saw a huge handle and a combination lock. The door and all the walls, behind the fabric, were metal. There was a large mirror on one wall. When she finished exploring she stood in one corner, gazing at the white couch, the only piece of furniture in the room. What alarmed her was that wherever she was it was something new, something that had not even been in the planning stage a year ago when she left All. She examined the floor. It was covered with a cheap piece of office carpeting that didn't stretch quite to the walls. Along one wall she noticed a long slit by the floorboard that looked like an air vent.

15

Joseph Cordite stopped outside of Eli's door to speak to Thomas. He restrained himself from commenting on the needlepoint canvas Thomas was clutching in his muscular hands. Prickles of hair were beginning to grow back on Thomas's shaved head, and it occurred to Cordite that Thomas had not been off duty for several days. He didn't want to replace him now, to expand the number of people who knew about Jeanette Burger. "How long has she been in there?" Cordite asked.

"Half hour."

Cordite nodded, patting him on the shoulder, and continued walking in his heavy, rolling pace, the change in his pockets jingling as he hitched up his pants and rounded the corner. At the end of this rather short hall there was a nondescript door which looked like it led to a broom closet. Cordite knocked on the door. When Dennis Blastrom opened it he had an excited smile on his face. "Oh, I'm glad you've arrived," Dennis said, pulling Cordite into the control room. "I'm ready to start now, as soon as she sits down!" He motioned to the large one-way mirror that hung above his instrument table. Cordite peered through the yellow glass and saw Jeanie pacing the small room, counting her steps, touching each corner as she turned. "She's nervous. I wish she'd sit down. If I start the humidifier working now she might fall and wonder where the bruises came from later. This preparation works in thirty seconds, she wouldn't have time to go down slow."

Cordite took the small drug company pamphlet on Pectaject (pectamine hydrochloride) that Dennis handed him, but he didn't look at it. "If the stuff is manufactured commercially what do we need you for?" he asked, patting Dennis's thin shoulder to show the question was asked in good humor.

Dennis turned away from the mirror, eager to answer. "That's the truth. Any doctor can administer this medication intravenously, but when the person comes to they know they've *had* something and discount all their mental reactions. But with this," he patted the cooling element on the humidifier onto which he had attached a jar of clear liquid, "first of all, she'll breathe it in so she won't know she had anything to stimulate the profound meditation experience. Second, I'm directing her experience by psychological means. Our theory is that psychological and pharmacological stimuli can be combined to achieve dramatic results. And the environment must be controlled too, which I guess you could say is what the Church of All is, a controlled environment. And third, I put some dimethyl sulfoxide in the solution so the drug will enter the bloodstream through the skin membranes and the—"

Cordite held up his hand for Dennis to stop. "I'm not going to remember this. Do you think you could write up a few notes for me. I gotta write a special report to the division. They're really on my ass. They think they can just ring up and say hey you guys have a problem with this Burger girl, and when I ask them for help in security they bounce the ball right back to us."

Dennis's goggle-shaped glasses danced on his rather oily nose. He reached under the table and hauled up an old

Royal typewriter. "I can write some notes while I'm working with her. Who do you have on security? Just Thomas?"

"Isn't he a winner? When these ex-Marines go soft they really go."

"Why don't you get some old reports for me so I can copy the format. I'll get something ready for the typist."

Cordite hitched up his pants and patted Dennis on the back. "Make it good, Dennis. They're already preparing a plausible denial and threatening to put the research program back in hospitals and prisons 'where it belongs.'"

"That's a bunch of crap. We have the ideal conditions here. They know it."

Cordite opened the door, but didn't step out, staring again at Jeanette, who was still pacing the experimental chamber. "I hope you're not going to knock her off in there. We don't need a corpse lying around the Reverence the day before the big rally."

Dennis sighed, consulting the drug company pamphlet. "I'd really like to keep a check on her blood pressure and respiration rate, but that would blow it. She'd remember that something had happened to her. But it says here: 'accidental administration of ten times the required dosage was followed by prolonged but complete recovery.' So don't worry."

"I worry. I'm going to move Thomas down here to guard this door. Eli's entrance is much more secure."

"Hey, don't do that. I never like to have this door guarded. It's inconspicuous—that's the best protection."

Cordite shrugged, closing the door. He walked down the hall and told Thomas to move his chair and his needlepoint around the corner and keep an eye on both corridors. He told him not to move from the spot, that he'd order his lunch sent up.

Dennis was glad to be alone again in his exciting control room. He sat down in front of the mirror, one arm leaning on the narrow table, the other resting on the button that could send up to sixteen gallons of vaporized chemical mixture into the experimental chamber he had had built to his own design specification by a plant in New Jersey. He was waiting for Jeanie to sit down on the white couch. Instead, she stood in the corner of the room, pulling on first one then another of her reddish brown curls. She was talking to herself, but not loudly enough for Dennis to pick up over the open microphone.

She had finished noting all the details of the small room. Her lips moved slowly as she rehearsed what she would say to Eddie Market when she finally emerged, child in arms, from what the newspapers would call a "chilling ordeal." She wished Zinger would hurry up, but Eli never hurried. It had been a thrill to see him again. She admired his grace, his words. That was the American problem, she thought, admiring winners. Even the communists can't help admiring their fellow opportunists who manage to defend civil rights cases and still have fancy suburban homes with expensive proletarian art on the walls and carpets from Third World countries.

She thought of Paul and the cup of his affection that was spilling over her life. It was as if the next chapter of her life was waiting impatiently to begin and all this was simply an annoying delay. Her legs grew tired of waiting and she let herself sink slowly to the floor. From that view she realized there was a shadow behind the large cloudy mirror. She stood up and leaned against the glass. She spoke loudly, beating out the words.

"If Leelannee and I are not out of here in a few hours the documents *and* the copies of checks from government agencies will be automatically mailed to a list of people in the media."

There was no response and the shadows behind the mirror did not move. Perhaps the shadows were furniture, not people. She sat down on the couch with her face in her hands.

A faint whirring sound began near the baseboard of the room. She felt a cool, damp breeze on her ankles. A weariness blew over her. She put her head on the arm of the couch and stretched out. Should kick off my shoes. Not nice, shoes on a white couch. She couldn't uncross her legs to kick off her shoes. She felt herself sloshing toward sleep. Not now. Why sleep now? Here? The damp breeze rose to her cheeks.

She was in a submarine sinking slowly to the oily black plants on the ocean floor. The whirring grew louder and the breeze shivered her body. She wanted a cover. She didn't want to hear the voice that bubbled toward her.

"Are we making contact, Jeanette? Nod your head if you hear these words."

She would not. She never did what she was told. Who knows why? It's much easier just to do what you're told and have reasonable desires. Fall in/left/right/about face. All the kids loved marching except her.

"Our spheres are touching, Jeanette. Don't try to speak. Nod your head. Do you know who I am?"

It wasn't Eli Zinger. There was no smoke or fire in the voice.

"Jeanette, trust me. I'm going to guide you back to yourself."

She tried to pry her eyes open to find the mouth of that voice. But the submarine was sealed tight as it sank slowly toward the ocean floor. She knew that voice. She had been in love with that voice and the thick lips that carried it into space. She didn't trust him. Dennis never liked to tell her where they were going. Cordite said she didn't have to go back with Dennis! Hold on to time. Don't surrender.

"You are entering the deepest meditation experience of

your many lives. Trust me. I will lead you back into orbit. Remember how you felt when you first saw Eli Zinger on that fall day at . . ."

I'll remember what I want to remember! The damp breeze moved over the years, shuffling them loosely. She had to remember something. She couldn't hold on to time. She was compelled to look for the sunken ship of truth on the ocean floor.

The breeze felt like the metallic thrill of sex. When sex slapped her in the face it almost knocked off the high hat of her I.Q. Sex had no respect for a high I.Q. Chapter one says you love him, love him with all your heart.

She couldn't hold on to time, couldn't uncross her legs to kick off her shoes. But she could remember what she wanted to remember. The metallic taste of sex.

Chapter two says you tell him, you're never never never never never gonna part.

She could talk to Dennis about everything. She was eighteen and there was no party being called *the party* in hushed tones of respect. She'd always thought there would be. She could talk to Dennis about that.

She talked to him in his car, a red car with springs squealing under the upholstery as she learned the taste of 100 miles, 500 miles, 1,000 miles, stopping only for gas and cardboard containers of coffee which they drank in the car so the lights of the restaurant wouldn't pierce the darkness of the night road. Sickness from the caffeine and artificial milk in their stomachs. Dennis was kissing her and digging his fingers into her panties. It felt so good. So good. "Not in the car, Dennis."

"We have to do it. You know that, Jeanie. In another month we'll both be in the looney bin."

"Not in the car, I couldn't stand it."

"Where do you want to go?"

"Somewhere with a bed, where no one will come."

"How about this motel, Jeanie? Seven dollars a night."

"No, not a motel."

"Why the hell not? We're right here!"

"You'd have to lie and say we were married. We could get caught. I don't want to lie." Her family never lied. They took the Fifth Amendment, but they'd never considered just lying and saying, no, I was never a member, or being defiant and saying, yes, yes, I was a member. . . .

"Christ!"

"Listen, Dennis, there's no hurry, we have plenty of time."

"Not in the car, not in the motel. What do you want me to do? Rent a palace?" He looked so cute in his black curly hair and his goggly smile and he was so intelligent. The high hat of his I.Q. probably towered over her own.

"Yes, a palace," she smiled, "with guards in red uniforms to keep back the intruders and a full orchestra playing passionate music in the next room." She poked his side. "Like in the movies."

He had to keep his anger down for fear she'd go back on her monumental decision to do it sometime, somewhere. He assumed she was what she pretended to be. He didn't know about the Trotskyite.

In chapter four you break up, but you give it just one more chance. She was seasick from all the coffee in cardboard containers. The cool breeze was all over. She needed a cover. The Trotskyite had covered her with political instruction while he groped for sex. She had to be careful. Once you start doing it with a guy you have to keep on doing it. It didn't kill her, didn't split her right open like she was afraid, but she had to keep on doing it, even though she liked the kissing part best. The Trotskyite's apartment was in a tenement way downtown in an abandoned building, where the only heat was from the gas burners on the stove. He had a rifle in the corner for shooting rats. She was seventeen. She had never seen an abandoned building before. His fingernails were edged with plaster from his job. He spoke about the years after the Russian revolution, when Trotsky and Stalin were locked in battle, as if he'd just heard something about it on a news bulletin. He was the first person to tell her she had a "background." She asked him to shut up about 1921 and fuck her. Then she had to keep on doing it, thinking about politics and why she had to spend the best years of her life in the 1950s instead of back when people had real parties and real causes to throw their lives into.

She had to keep on doing it until the day he stopped calling her. Later she found out he was in a fancy mental hospital on Fifth Avenue. He had robbed a taxi cab with the rifle he kept for shooting rats. Why would he? Why would he rob a taxi driver? It made her chilled to think about it. "I asked the driver for *half* his money," he told her later. "I'm a socialist, a working man myself, I told him to give me half, put the rest back in his pocket, and tell the boss I got it all." She thought about the poor taxi driver trembling with a rifle at his head while he counted out half the money. At least it let her off the hook. She could stop doing it and she vowed she wouldn't start again.

After the Trotskyite, Dennis seemed so light.

"You'll never guess where we're going," he said. It was their sophomore year at college. They had three weeks of intersession before them. They were in his car. It was snowing.

"Florida?" she said. "Fort Lauderdale!"

"No, no." He was smiling with his eyes on the road, and he never did tell her where they were going.

It was symptomatic! she thought suddenly, rising above the whirring noise and the gray-green ocean that sloshed in her stomach. He didn't like to tell her where they were going. If she truly loved and trusted him, then she didn't need to know. What was the matter with her? Didn't she love him enough? Why did she need to know?

He parked the car in front of a building on Twentieth Street, opened the lobby door with a key, and led her up three flights of stairs. He opened the door to an apartment. It was empty except for a single bed that lay against one wall.

"What?"

He closed the door behind her. He took a transistor radio out of a paper bag he was carrying and put it on the windowsill. The news came on. Then a babble of commercials. She stood listening to the radio as if an important announcement was due any minute.

He smiled from across the room. "No one will bother us. The snow won't snow on us. The rent is seventy dollars a month and I split it with Terry. We get to use it every other night and on alternate weekends."

"Where are the sheets?"

"Sheets? I don't know about sheets." He had his hands on her shoulders, pushing her down on the naked mattress. "This is it, kid, don't tell me about sheets."

"And a pillow. We can't do it without a pillow."

He lay his head on her stomach and that felt good. She looked up at the cracked yellow ceiling.

Who, whooo wrote the book of love?

Dennis went down to the car to bring up a sleeping bag. What the hell. She had to do it again with someone sooner or later.

He threw the sleeping bag open on the bed and they spent some time looking at the pattern: brown bears climbing trees. His face was white. His body was brittle. Jeanie turned off the light and kicked off her shoes and lay next to him.

"Do you love me, Jeanie?"

Who wrote the book . . .

"Yes." It was only polite, at a time like that. Should she

ask him if he loves her? Why push it? "You never did this before, did you Dennis?"

"No. Did you?"

"Uh huh."

"Well, good." He laughed.

"It's just like a freezing lake," she laughed, relieved that he was laughing, "terrible until you jump in, but once you get warmed up it's not so bad."

He laughed and she laughed and the bears climbed up the trees on the sleeping bag and stuck their hands in a hive for some honey and licked it up with a grin.

It wasn't as bad as with the Trotskyite, but she still liked the kissing part best. If he got so absorbed in fucking that he stopped kissing her it became terrible, like riding around the corner of the overpass and getting slapped in the face by sex. Once she started doing it with Dennis she might as well get married and get out of that horrible room. If they got married she'd be free to quit college and find something significant to throw her life into.

Once, only for a moment, the submarine stopped sinking and the whirring sound quieted, and she tried to pick her fingers up off the floor. She tried so hard that her hand flew up above her head and her body twitched and turned. She lay there watching her fingers fly above her face. She could see her fingers quite clearly even though her eyes were closed.

16

Dennis peered at the mirror, then checked the gauge on the humidifier to see how much of the chemical solution had vaporized into the room. Jeanie did not look heavily anesthetized. Her arms and legs jerked in tonic, seizurelike spasms. Dennis was tempted to increase the speed with which the drugs were vaporized into the room, but he hesitated and once more read through the drug company's leaflet until he found a note that tonic and clonic seizures were an infrequent, adverse reaction to pectamine, but did not imply a light plane.

He opened the microphone. "Jeanette, trust me. I will help you find your way back to yourself. You need a guide to the unknown territories of your mind. Do you trust me? Nod your head."

She trusted him. She was in love with that voice. She was sure of it. But he never wanted to tell her where they were going. If he wouldn't tell her where they were going she wouldn't nod her head left/right/left/right. He wouldn't tell her what he put in Leelannee's bottle that time to make her fall asleep without crying. She kept the bottles away from him. Was Leelannee sick? Her stomach was cold and she tried to hold it, but her arms remained twitching above her head.

"Let me locate you, Jeanette. Vancouver Island. Going across by ferry to meet Eli Zinger and Faye and the experiences that changed our entire lives? Nod your head if you're located in the right sphere."

Dennis turned off the mike, deciding to wait and see if the tonic spasms died down before increasing the dosage of pectamine and DMSO. He had prepared much more of the mixture than he thought would be necessary. He had a lot of hope for this formula. From the beginning of his association with Eli Zinger he had pumped various substances into the meditation room with steadily improving results. But most of the followers were more than willing to relive their conversion experience; they hungered after religious sensation; they could get high from the scent of jasmine, as Dennis was fond of saying. Whereas Jeanette Burger was impatient with religious experiences. She had attended the meditation room, even in the best of times, with great reluctance and seemed annoyed, rather than ecstatic, each time her initial conversion enthusiasm was restored. Dennis was convinced it was Eli's leniency, in permitting Jeanie to skip meditation, that caused her break with All in the first place. Eli used to say if he wasn't sure of Jeanette he wasn't sure of anyone.

A sharp rap on the door broke into Dennis's thoughts. He checked that the microphone was off and opened the hallway door. Cordite stood talking to Thomas Baker, who had moved his chair and his needlepoint directly outside Dennis's control room. Dennis let Cordite in and closed the door. "I thought I asked you to keep Thomas away from my door. Any Church member who passes is going to know something interesting is going on here now."

"Oh, I have to keep him away from Helena Carpenter," Cordite said. "If Eli sees that little bitch flirting with Thomas . . ."

"Is that what she's up to now?" Dennis laughed. "She's the first girl who hasn't had the decency to wait until Eli is through with her to start fucking around."

Cordite pulled a rolled up bunch of paper from his back pocket, slapping it back and forth between his hands. "I brought you these reports."

Dennis nodded. Cordite leaned over the control table and looked in on Jeanie. "How you doing?"

"Fine."

"You think she's ready to take phone calls?"

"Phone calls? This isn't instant change. You gotta give me at least a couple more hours."

"The phone's been ringing off the hook for her. Her parents, lawyers, newsmen, people from some dingbat coalition. She has a lotta friends."

"You can stall them off for a while," Dennis said. "In a

couple more hours she can talk to her parents and tell them she's decided to re-enter on a trial basis . . . she'll be very convincing. Remember Alley McDonald?"

"Sure I remember. He's your masterpiece, Dennis. Hard-nosed reporter converts! But this one. If she weren't your wife . . ."

Dennis tensed, opening the door. "Come back in a couple of hours, Joseph. And take"—he jerked his pointed chin in Thomas's direction—"him away from the door before you start a whole round of rumors."

"How come I never hear the rumors that go around this place?" Cordite hitched up his pants, suddenly dropping several coins on the blue rug, which Thomas picked up.

"You want to know what the latest rumor is?" Dennis smiled, leaning against the doorway. "I heard it from the girls in the nursery when I brought Leelannee in. The latest word is that the CIA has penetrated—that's a direct quote—penetrated the Church of All with a very cleverly disguised agent. When I asked who she thought this agent was the first thing she said was, 'Well, not Mr. Cordite, that would be just too obvious.' "

Cordite was not smiling as broadly as Dennis. "I think when you get Jeanette back in line a lot of this wild speculation will stop." He waited until Dennis closed the door, then told Thomas to remain at his post until he returned.

The tonic spasms in Jeanie's legs had subsided, and only one arm now jerked above her head. Dennis pushed the control on the humidifier from slow to medium, increasing the flow of the vaporized drugs into the sealed meditation chamber. Almost immediately Jeanie's arm dropped to her chest and her whole body seemed to repose. Dennis timed five minutes, made some notes in the black and white hard-covered notebook, then pushed the button back to slow and opened the microphone.

"Are you located, Jeanie? Shake your head, yes or no? Can you see Eli Zinger now, see him as you first saw him?" Dennis waited a while, but Jeanie did not stir her head or show any signs of hearing the questions. This puzzled him. Alley McDonald had freely answered all questions when he was under pectamine; he had even spoken a few words. It was possible, of course, that she was having the desired experiences and just unable to shake her head, but it worried Dennis. He didn't want to exceed the safety limits. He didn't want to harm her. He wanted her to shake her head, gently, yes and no, and become again the girl who had loved him so enthusiastically.

She wouldn't give him the satisfaction, even though her chin and jaw ached from the effort of not nodding her head. She didn't know which was worse: when he didn't tell her where they were going, or when he told her and she was powerless to do anything but follow.

"Where are we going Dennis?"

"West."

"Where west?"

" 'Cross Canada. You'll see."

The breeze swept her like a current. She could no longer choose what to remember, she could just barely manage not to nod her head. The memory he evoked was filled with sunshine and shadows and smelled of the woods. But it was something she preferred to forget.

They were as far west as you could get by car, so they took a ferry. It was not her idea of a beautiful place. In some areas the vegetation was so thick and blue that if you managed to fight your way in, the bushes could steal the knife right off your belt. There was a strange, long sweep of ocean without the craggy nooks of the familiar Atlantic. Harsh yellow bushes and hurricane-bent pines. It felt like the end of the world. All she really wanted to do was turn east.

Yes, it was nice that Eli Zinger, of all people, had become a star and got his picture on the cover of *Viewer* magazine. She had once met him on Sixth Avenue when she was playing hookey from school. So they had an excuse to knock on the side of his flat-roofed cabin, as if an excuse was needed in this ragged camp of stoned-out refugees from Los Angeles.

A young woman pushed aside the Indian bedspread that served as a door and stepped out into the sunlight, naked. She embraced Jeanie for a long long time until Jeanie stopped watching Dennis's surprised face and sank into the large breasts, accepting the embrace. It was an endlessly prolonged sensation, like sinking into the cool breeze of memory.

Faye took them inside and they sat near the easel where Eli Zinger was painting. "I drew your portrait once," he said to Jeanie. "I don't remember your name, but I remember you gave me a veal cutlet sandwich in payment. It was the only thing I ate that day. It had lettuce on it." He laughed loudly from deep under his beard. "You must stay for supper, I owe you a meal."

"They're gonna stay for the rest of their lives," Faye said. "I feel it."

"Don't be nervous, Jeanie." Dennis put his arm around her. "We don't have any plans for the rest of our lives anyway." The instant acceptance thrilled him. There were no qualifications, stipulations, exemptions, applications. Jeanie wanted to turn east, right then.

Eli sent the rest of the commune members to cut firewood in the forest; the rangers had marked some trees for thinning. It was autumn and the air was perfect.

She heard Dennis asking her to nod her head, and rolled it against the back of the couch so it would stay still. The breeze grew quieter. She tried to lift her fingers off the floor.

"Do some acid, do some mescaline," Eli said. Said. Eli sent out sound waves that tingled in her brain and brought back a surge of consent. From Dennis too. From Jeanie, who was not wary, but glad these drugs had been invented before she got too old to enjoy them, glad the fifties had yielded to times when anything could happen.

They swallowed a big tablet, the color of a purple jellybean, then rose and parted. Dennis went out to walk. Eli swept the worn Oriental carpet. Faye sneaked off into the kitchen to drink some milk. She told Jeanie to keep it quiet, that Eli did not approve of milk.

"Why?"

"Oh, it gives phlegm or something. I'm not sure. Eli knows."

Jeanie ran out to the barn where the people who went to cut wood had been living. How could Faye worry about drinking milk but not about filling her blood with mescaline during pregnancy? It seemed to Jeanie a very brave act. Gambling with the future of the human race. A gamble was necessary. To bring up another generation as lost and flaccid as she and Dennis . . . or to risk and risk for decades and then sell out in one stroke like her parents. She found a matted paperback in the barn.

It was two hours before she felt anything. Then she felt a tug on her brain, a slight tug, like the call of a houseplant in need of water. The print of the book became bolder and bolder. Each word enlarged to half the page as if she held a huge magnifying glass before her eye. She read on, eyes moving from giant word to giant word until the word LOVE hit her in the eye and tore her attention away from the sentence. She got up and went outside. Her eye magnified each object. A caterpillar with red-brown fur crawling up the doorstep. Cloud visible in the night sky. She felt good. She liked this part of tripping. Knowing she was on a drug, seeing the things she was always supposed to be looking at.

Knowing she was on a drug. Knowing. She tried to lift her fingers off the floor. She tried to know but the past was stronger than the present.

Feet stepping from stone to stone in the driveway. A cool breeze through the tunnel of her instep. Feet having an orgasm in intercourse with stone. Don't tell anyone about it. The conversation convention is canceled. The how are you and how do you do.

If her feet could feel all this, what about other bodily surfaces? She's not one of those dolls with her clothes sewed onto her stuffing. She is feet in love with the wind. The wind wants her dress, knocking it between her knees. If she could see Dennis, he would talk to the wind about her dress. A conversation convention could be arranged with all due promptitude. The elastic from her dress seizes her waist. She has to breathe. Who could argue about breathing? She pulled the dress up over her head and hung it on a tree branch. She pulled the bikini panties down her endlessly long legs and tossed the coil of nylon like a frisbee onto her sleeping bag. The wind washed her skin and she trembled and felt as weak as the cloud moving away to the other end of the sky. When the moon comes out—why anticipate? The wind asked the question, not her. Isn't it enough for you? The wind washing your body and a dim red star pulsating in the night with messages from other universes. A drug is technology, Eli Zinger said in bold type in *Viewer* magazine, a technical improvement of the brain cells that can be programmed for good or evil. When the moon comes out she will see the difference between good and evil. Why anticipate?

Is she hot or cold? Does she need a cover? Can she lift her fingers off the floor?

She stretched her arms up to touch the top of the doorway. If she's hot she can run out in the wind. If she's cold she can dive into her sleeping bag and cuddle with the brown bears. She knows she's *something.*

She is not the only god in the heavens. She is not the only revolutionary impulse. She is not the only receptacle of visionary wisdom. Messages tug at her brain. Her skull is growing. The body without clothes simply went the way of all flesh. Her skull is swelling; the bones slowly separating to make way for more gray mass. Her hair is thinning in a sense of expansion. A new cloud appears on the horizon. Cloud clearing a path for the moon. Her jawbone feels the weight of each individual tooth. Side effects.

She turned her body in toward the barn. The wind showered on her back. What a busy world, this barn. Spider webs hanging off the moldings and the floor crawling with wood grains. All this scene in the light of the kerosene lantern that is smoking black and evil around the lips of the glass. Lower the lantern. Jeanette Burger strode to the lantern and turned the brass knob. The lowered flame stopped smoking. She saw her act was good. She released herself again. Don't leave the lantern burning when you leave the barn. Those were her final words, as she shed her earthly persona and became the goddess.

The goddess lay down with the brown bears in the sleeping bag. Her eyes closed from the crawling wood grains. Eli Zinger's purple jellybean had opened a door on the universe. Her godship twisted on the bed, sending off a pink and iridescent blue aura which expanded until the room was filled with other-terrestrial light.

If she were a goddess she could fly. Don't jump to conclusions. Jeanette hung on to her body, debating the goddess, refusing to be completely shed. Don't jump out a fourth-story window. The great truth of the body/spirit split must be remembered. Jeanette was a materialist; her godship was not so sure. Beware of early enthusiasms, you convert, you. All revolutionaries are materialists. Only the unimaginative ones.

The goddess triumphed. Philosophy, like colors, crawling wood grains, is not of the essence. Go out and check on the cloud clearing a path for the moon. Before her godship left the barn she slowly turned the brass knob on the lantern, holding her breath and praying for safety as she plunged herself into darkness. It was the first time she ever prayed. Then, with a sigh, even the graven image of the goddess was transcended.

It stepped out into the night as only an Egg, skull without hair and two long skinny legs wobbling under the weight of all that gray matter engaged in wave communication with the surfaces of the earth. Bloop de bloop. There were sharp stones under its feet. Damp dark grass between its toes. The window of the cabin smiled with light. Egg was perfect; but it needed something; fire?

Eli Zinger moved out of the cabin to serve the Egg. He lay the small sticks first, then the larger ones, criss-cross, criss-cross, and flames leaped out of the cold ashes as he blew. Jean/her godship/the Egg needed that fire, needed the firemaker.

"Your wish is my command" is the thought that flew between the two minds. Eli left the Egg. It sat praising the leaping flames, smiling over the alligator hide of orange squares glowing on the log.

Where are you? the thought flew out of the woods. This way Dennis.

A witch with dark hair ran out of the cabin and around the fire. The Egg watched the witch. The witch was consumed with otherness, passiön, desire for something outside herself. The Egg wondered at this. It, too, needed something.

A man ran out of the woods toward the fire. When a fire is lit the people on the planet come toward it. His chest was marbled with red lines. He bent over the Egg.

"How are you feeling?"

The double power of sound and meaning almost cracked the Egg before it was ready to be born. It recovered and tapped its forehead with some fingers that were lying on its knees.

If she could do that now . . . if she could lift her fingers off the floor.

The man looked at the cabin. "Should we go in?"

The Egg trembled at the word we. A moment of rage. We? It and this man with war paint on his chest? He was not what the Egg needed. But his eyes were kind beneath his glasses. The Egg knew a time had come. Change had come. The man helped it stand up and slowly as slowly could be they rolled into the doorway of the house.

Inside the witch sat with her desire by her side. Eli climbed up the loft and unhinged a painting, leaping back to the floor. He rolled up the painting and gave it to Jeanette/her godship/the Egg. The Egg started to nod, but even a nod was unnecessary. They were in the territory of the unutterable, where communication was perfect.

Who was she when the moon came out? This question would later be debated as the great turning point in their marriage.

It was her godship who rose and went outside. The twitter of the night insects told her that the moon had surfaced in the ocean of the night. She went outside and raised her naked arms, extending her pink and blue iridescence to the white excitement of the moon.

Eli was close behind her, full of intent. She felt his intent more than his fingers or his beard. His arms moved around her and held her breasts with such a full and skinful feeling that her godship fled, thinking, he will not love me as well as the wind.

It was time for the chick to be born. And like every born thing it was born with sex: female. Female? There was no doubt about it the way Eli was slowly dipping his finger in and out of her squeaky hole and she leaned back on him so not to fall.

A man can always remember where to go and what to do no matter how stoned he is. Eli heard her inner laugh and laughed out loud, for he too was being reborn and discovering his sex at birth. He led her to the barn, to the sleeping bag, and opened her with his fingers and pushed his tipped penis into her. Her womb started gushing to soothe the friction. They rocked and rested together. It was not making love, she later explained to Dennis, it was a meeting of the spheres.

After much time had passed the drug level in her brain dropped. Suddenly, they were not as stoned as they had been. They rolled apart on the sleeping bag. Eli leaned on one elbow and looked at her. He was going to speak. The first words to be spoken as the dawn leaped into the room were: "I'm glad our life paths have crossed again."

She had to reply, because she did want a conversation. But what reply? "What the fuck do you mean, life paths?"

Eli was startled, offended, then at last something broke in his aura. "What do you want from me? Why did you come looking for me? Hundreds of people are looking for me, and they all want something from me they can only find in themselves."

She crossed her legs and felt her shrunken body quite under control. "We just came here because we read in a magazine that you'd come up with a way of living that was worth something." It was quite easy to talk once she got the hang of it.

"I have, Jeanette."

"You have? This place looks like what the poverty program is helping people in West Virginia get away from." A long sentence like that, with meaning attached too.

"Don't be deceived by externals. When we need money, we will have money. Now we need pioneers to scout new territory, to lead the people toward cataclysmic change." He put his hand on her knee. She stroked his beard. "And what is your life about, Jean?"

She had it ready. Synopsis of life past, prepared and prerecorded on the car ride up to Vancouver. "Quit school, got married, got an apartment, got a job, got this job where I'm easier to replace than a typewriter ribbon and less expensive. Got furniture, going to get better furniture, maybe have a kid if Dennis ever finishes school, maybe go to Florida for a vacation. Wear clothes, don't go naked, take drugs only on weekends, eat meat, don't fuck our friends, watch TV. Big discussions about the meaning of life. Conclusion: make me a sandwich. Big discussions about how to change society. Conclusion: don't bother. Wake up every morning wondering why I'm waking up, why I'm going to work. Conclusion: pay the rent."

Eli was not laughing, though she felt this was the cleverest speech she had ever made in her twenty years of life. He rested his hands on the top of her head. "You see it. I was the same as that. I just stepped out of it. I want a revolution in *my* lifetime. I live in places where I don't have to pay the rent."

They felt a noise and a presence. "Here comes the landlord," Eli said.

Dennis stood in the doorway until they flapped their

hands for him to come. He sat down on the corner of the sleeping bag. She saw the war paint on his chest was hundreds of deep scratches. "Does it hurt?"

"I was running in the woods last night."

"Do you think we can sleep now?" she asked no one but the drug inside her. The barn was full of light and in the clutter on the floor she saw eggshell pieces and an iridescent scarf left behind by her godship. They let her sleep.

In the morning it was all arranged. He didn't even want to tell her, but Eli Zinger insisted that everyone enter All with full awareness. So Dennis was waiting at the foot of her sleeping bag when she woke up, and he told her they were staying in Vancouver.

She rubbed her eyes and looked around the barn. It was very messy. The wood grains still crawled if she stared at them too long. "What the hell are we going to do here?"

He nodded, his glasses dancing on his nose, as if that were just the kind of obvious, uninspired question he could expect from someone like her. "Eli has work for me to do."

"Oh yeah? What about your Ph.D.?"

"The work of All is more important. More exciting."

"What's the project?"

She talked as if it were a real job, with a goal and a paycheck, instead of a submersion.

"You had a powerful experience last night?"

She reached up to touch her skull and was surprised at its smallness. She was very sensitive to the sounds Dennis was making; they ran through her and seemed full of significance she couldn't quite grasp. "Yes, powerful," she said, accepting his inadequate word at last.

"You'll never have that again."

"What?"

"No matter how much acid or mescaline you take, you'll never again have an experience as powerful as when you first realize that God lives in you and that you're connected to all mankind."

Jeanie nodded doubtfully. "I'll never have it again?"

"Not with the drugs we have now. Eli just explained it to me."

"Well, that's okay, I'm not sure I want it again."

Dennis stood up, clenching his hands in frustration. "You're the most uncooperative . . . Why the hell did we get married? So you could purposely misconstrue and misunderstand everything I say."

Why the hell did they get married? It was a valid enough question, it was just that she didn't have the head for it at the moment. "Go on, Dennis, finish."

He paced in tight circles. "Maybe you don't want to re-experience the transcendence of that experience . . . Or maybe you're just still coming down . . . But most other human beings on this planet . . . Why do all these communes and socialist experiments being set up fail? They fail because the people can't keep up that initial spirit. . . ."

Eli Zinger stood in the doorway. His beard and hair looked yellow in the morning light. He was a pleasure to look at.

"I see you talked my husband into staying," Jeanie called.

Eli nodded, smiling. "Now I've come for you." He looked at Dennis, calmly, affectionately, until of his own free will Dennis rose and left them alone. Jeanie turned her back to him and pulled on her dungarees and workshirt. Then she walked toward him and they strolled into the bright autumn morning.

"What's it all about?" she asked lazily. "I slept with you, so he feels he has to do something dramatic?"

Eli was about a head taller than Jeanie; she felt a rush of the remaining drug each time she lifted her chin to look at him.

"I need him," Eli said. "I need you, too. I need you even more."

"To tend the chickens? Do you have chickens here? I never liked animals very much."

He laughed out loud, for a long time. "I need you for the jokes, for one thing. So far I've been attracting the very serious Zen Buddhist types. But that will change."

The wind was showering through the trees and the grass was sparkling at her feet. Surely she had noticed that sound and that sparkle before, but it all seemed very new. Eli's voice came in a rush, like the sound of the wind through the leaves. "The special job I have for you, Jeanette, is the war in Vietnam."

She looked up at him, startled because she had been expecting something womanly, something related to the rocking and resting of the night before.

"There's a tendency here not to connect to the outer world. Some of their godships don't want to permit newspapers and radios, and while I agree that they should not be disturbed, I think someone must keep track. I think All must do its part to protest the war."

She looked down at the grass sparkling at her feet. She hadn't thought there was anything he could say to make her stay here with the chickens. But he had managed to find the thing.

17

Dennis's sigh had a low whistle to it. He consulted his stopwatch and made a notation in his black and white hardcover notebook. He checked the level of liquid in the humidifier. He was about to turn to other things, when he decided to check on Jeanette one more time.

"All is ready for you. Are you ready for All? Nod . . ."

She nodded emphatically, tossing her damp curls about her cheeks, nodding and nodding, until the sight of her frizzy hair shaking annoyed Dennis and he said: "You can stop nodding now," into the microphone. The nodding wound down, little by little, until her cheek rested against her shoulder. She looked like a girl who had been drowned in a river then left by the fast-moving current to dry out among the brambles on the banks. The high humidity in the experimental chamber had brought a polished ivory sheen to her cheeks, and the stray red hairs were like veins fringing her face. Dennis thought she looked beautiful whenever her body was at rest, free from the tonic jerks and excessive nodding. Beautiful when wet. The dampness made her seem accessible, unlike her usual abrupt self with a mousetrap mind, as Dennis called it. He thought of turning up the humidifier to high speed and going to lie down next to her on the couch and enjoy the high. But without the psychological stimulus, he might go astray. Of course he could always play one of the tapes that guided the average follower through the meditation sessions.

He stopped dreaming and turned to the report Cordite had given him. He pulled the old Royal typewriter near him and inserted a paper. He should remember to ask Cordite for one of those new typewriters he could just record into. Cordite was very generous with equipment. He might fret about Faye's orders for jewelry, but he never bucked on an invoice for electronic equipment. That was obviously useful, even if it just replaced last year's model.

Dennis pecked out a few lines and marked where the changes should be made in the last quarterly report. He concentrated on the section headed "Paramilitary Methods." The

Church of All as an agency of gray propaganda and crowd control didn't interest him. That was Eli Zinger's department; it had been Jeanette's department too before she abruptly decided that All had turned 180 degrees from its original purpose. Dennis thought she was wrong about that. All had not rotated, merely shifted with the times and bent to external pressures. The Church of All was surviving, which was more than you could say about the other new forms that had been born in the late 1960s. To Dennis, gray propaganda and crowd control were simply public relations. He was interested in the technical improvements that could bring one person, one person at a time, to re-experience conversion: that moment when Eli Zinger offered them the one thing in life they had always wanted.

Dennis had finished typing out the description of his latest drug combination and made careful indications about where the typist was to insert it into the old report, when he realized that a noise was bothering him. He began to check his equipment hastily. But the sound was not from the control room but from outside; it was a telephone ringing and ringing way down the hall. He opened the door and stared at Thomas Baker, who was sucking on his lower lip and working on his needlepoint. "Would you answer the telephone?"

"I can't. I mean I did," Thomas said. "I took it off the hook."

"But it's still ringing," Dennis said.

"Yes, they all are. All the ones on this floor. They're all off the hook and they're still ringing. The whole system's out of order."

Dennis pushed his glasses back on his nose. "I never heard of that before." The ringing was annoying him now with its intermittent persistence. "You mean you can't make it stop?"

"I can pull the phone out of the wall or cut the wire," he said, "but Cordite said to hold on, that the phone company is sending a repair crew right over."

The lights in the hall dimmed suddenly, then restored. Dennis was not sure it had happened. He went back into the control room where now, even with the door closed, he was painfully aware of the telephone ringing outside. The second time the lights dimmed he knew it had happened because the humidifier whirred to a stop, then started up again. Dennis dashed out of the room. "Tell Cordite there's a problem with the power. I must hook up the emergency generator."

Thomas nodded and began to contact Cordite on his walkie-talkie. Dennis returned to the mirror and stared in at Jeanette. The emergency generator had arrived last week but he hadn't had a chance to hook it up, so busy was he with policy decisions about Jeanette, plans for tomorrow's rally, and keeping Eli Zinger functioning through his period of unusually high epileptic activity. He twisted in his swivel chair, stood up, then bolted from the control room and ran down the hall without bothering to close the door. When he reached the telephone he began to pull on the line to pull it out of the wall. The lights dimmed. He stopped pulling on the wire, glancing upward, and the lights came back on. Thomas Baker was beside him by this time.

"Cordite said to wait on that, your godship."

"I can't stand it. I have work to do."

Thomas nodded and took the cord from Dennis's hand. With one firm yank he made the ringing stop. Dennis leaned against the wall, sweat running down from his hairline. They could hear the faint ring of telephones from other parts of the floor and perhaps beyond. "Is his godhead in his room?" Dennis asked.

Thomas's eyes were as blank as his bald skull. He annoyed Dennis because he was so unexpressive Dennis couldn't guess what went on in his head. "His godship is receiving," he said slowly.

"Who?" Dennis asked, and then, when he didn't answer: "It's important."

"Helena."

Dennis nodded and rounded the corner to knock on Eli's door. There was no answer. He put his ear to the highly arched door. There was a sound of a telephone ringing. Dennis knocked again. "We're having some equipment trouble," he called out.

Cordite leaned his heavy arm across Dennis's shoulders. "Take it easy." He walked him toward the control room. Cordite's pocket bulged with a wire cutter, which jangled against coins when he walked.

Thomas was bent over his needlepoint. The door to the control room was open and Dennis hurried inside and opened the carved wooden box from India where he kept his private collection. He did not usually open the box when he was experimenting, afraid of destroying his objectivity. But the telephones ringing faintly in the distance were traveling up his spinal column and he felt pain each time he turned his neck. He took a red and a yellow pill. That would make a nice balance. He was an ancient medicine man administering spiritual and natural cures. He instructed his body to restore itself and adapt to the new environmental conditions. After swallowing the pill with an air of ritual, he rested his head in his hands like Eli did, and tried to find a level of concentration below the ringing of the telephones.

Cordite opened the door. "How long is it going to take to hook up the generator?"

"No time at all. As soon as you get it up here."

Cordite glanced at Jeanette sprawled on the white couch looking half drowned by humidity. "Is she all right?"

"She's almost finished. I want Eli to go in and wake her up, but he isn't answering the door."

"He's downstairs instructing the followers about the rally and how to deal with the demonstration some group has mounted outside."

"Really? Thomas said he was receiving Helena in his room."

Cordite snorted, hitching up his pants. "That guy needs a rest."

"Who's demonstrating outside?"

"Beats me. Something about the national crisis, price hikes, profits. . . . I don't know what made them decide to picket us."

18

The breeze stopped. The air hung in damp silence. The whirring sound had stopped. Jeanie's ears were full of silence as if her face had broken through the surface of the ocean, broken through the underwater roar into the misty silence of space. She tried to lift her fingers off the floor and they bounced right up and landed neatly on her chest. She didn't know if her eyes were open or closed. She was very very glad it was so quiet now and that the breeze had stopped blowing on her cheeks. She was very very glad but she was worried about something. What was she worried about? Her fingers made small jerky motions around her face, searching for the fear. Had they managed to find Leelannee and take her back to Gail's? The question went off in her brain in red and yellow spiked lines. Or was that the overhead electric light that went on? The light danced in spikes before her eyes, which were open, which she closed with a frown. The whirring sound started up slowly. Paul. Of everything that she wanted—silence, air without breeze, darkness—she was reaching hardest for Paul as she slowly sank down down in the gray-green water until her toes touched the slimy black plants on the bottom of the ocean.

He was telling her what to remember. She was glad he did not tell her to nod because she was seasick in the throat and nodding was a great effort. Remembering was not a great effort. Remembering was as easy as a can of Bugler tobacco, blended Turkish and domestic, 7 oz. net wt., sitting next to a long package of Spiritual Sky, 20 long-burning, Bengali Lime incense sticks. Dennis's overalls and her long orange skirt hung on nails. She had dried flowers tied with string hanging upside down. She had white potholders with red crocheted roses. Dennis put a white candle in a green wine bottle with the label scrubbed off. Leelannee's baby clothes, folded and sorted, smelled of sunshine. She looked around her and deduced that she was happy.

He told her to remember, but did he? Did he really remember that can of Bugler tobacco on the dresser or was he merely lipping off again about spiritual values? It was hard to tell. His voice was uncommonly calm. He must be on something. Dennis was never naturally calm. Even after orgasm the first thing he wanted was a smoke, a sandwich, a shower, a brisk conversation. She was the one who liked to loll around. And she was lolling now. Lolling and remembering and trying, in her own little way, to avoid remembering.

Grab hold tightly, let go lightly. In those days Eli Zinger really did give spiritual instruction to those who wanted it. Jeanie never wanted it. How could she? It reminded her too much of the day she went to watch Sally make her First Communion in a little white bride's dress and white gloves that had tiny pearl buttons and loops at the wrist. Sally and her mother, all dressed up, entering the midnight blue cavern of the Immaculate Conception Church where candles flickered near the altar, and Jewish communist kids in red jackets and jeans stood outside, afraid to enter.

It was a stance, Eli told her. She set herself apart from the rest of the Vancouver commune. She defined herself as nonspiritual. Grab hold tightly, let go lightly. Don't stand apart. In Tao we trust. She made a feeble grab for it, looking foolish. Then Eli Zinger had his great insight into the specialized nature of the one hundred and fifty human beings that were now his great responsibility. In Tao we trust. Each has his way. Each has her way. We go our ways but we go together.

Jeanette's way was alongside Eli Zinger, zigzagging off and on the path to confront him with himself. She was intimate with him in a special way, unlike his wife and new initiates who became his mistresses for a while until they were subdued. She knew more about his past than others did, especially Dennis, and she enjoyed that. Dennis was always trying to drag information out of Eli as they walked, the five or six in the leadership cluster, on their morning tour of the sprawling commune. What kind of a kid were you, Eli? Dennis asked him. Did you play baseball? When did you first smoke pot? What were you doing the day John Kennedy was killed? Did you ever paint your name on the side of a building? Were you ever arrested? Are you now or have you ever been a member of the communist party?

"Not unless Jeanette has signed me up," Zinger smiled. He stretched tall and skinny as they looked over the acres of unpromising farm land. "When's that antiwar rally, Jeanette? Is it next Saturday? What have you arranged."

She had arranged for him to speak, which was a coup, for

neither the radicals nor the church pacifists liked Eli Zinger or the All commune. She had promised to bring all commune members to the demonstration. She had arranged for buses. She was at peace with herself, as they looked out at the muddy, rocky, hilly, brushy land they would till for the first time this year. It was the first year of commune life; their anniversary was that June. Things were beginning to wear out, she noticed, and Dennis's frayed and patched jeans were barely holding together.

It was as if Eli sifted her thoughts out of the air itself. "Culture is arbitrary," he said, to Jeanette, to Dennis, to Faye, to the other leaders who stood looking out on the rutted farm land. "We need to invent new forms, new words, new meanings, new diets, and new work patterns."

"And new drugs," Dennis added.

Eli smiled. "And a new manner of obedience."

There was no one else on the windswept field, and the air had an ocean freshness, for on Vancouver Island they were never too far from the sea.

Jeanie was scared of the new things. Each moment she was counting up the balance sheet and assuring herself things were all right. They sat on the floor, wore their hair long and straggly, dressed in cheap Indian cottons that twisted and shrank in the wash. They didn't resemble the middle class in the least. You couldn't find a polyester skirt or a plastic rain hat on the whole commune. That was good. Today they were fighting back, too. Eli Zinger would be speaking at an antiwar rally. The new field would be tilled so food wouldn't be as scarce this winter as it was last. That was all right. But the new culture? What if she didn't like it any better than she'd liked the city world of Hatchet-Faced Landlords, FBI men in the lobby, and sex slapping and slapping her across the face.

"You will like it," Zinger said to her. "You will all like the new things. You will invent them."

But sometimes the things she invented didn't please her, and the things she chose displeased her after a little while.

Zinger rested his hand on top of her head. "The old things are worn out. We have to invent new things."

He was right. Her slippers had worn out and there were no others. She wore socks but longed for her special expensive furry slippers. Long for slippers? If she started longing for slippers she'd start longing for shrimp fried rice and clock radios and shelves full of paperback books. Still, the socks were scratchy, and the commune had to make money. It was possible to survive, to be self-sufficient to a large degree, with one hundred fifty people farming and building and caring for the young. It just wasn't that interesting, especially for one like Jeanie whose brain chewed over everything until it was a soggy pulp of meaning. She wished she had some books to chew over.

She stood looking out at the field after the other leaders had moved away. She reflected. She was very thoughtful all through that first year, and asked Dennis for a little something whenever the urge to be more active snapped up at her. The mud didn't smell nice. It was like spoiled pudding. The breeze had stopped for a moment and the air seemed to heat up, like air that had been breathed many times before. She wished she had a book, or a newspaper. Something to move her reflections away from the fantastic turn her life had taken that landed her in the rocky muddy country that they all said was so beautiful. Eli Zinger was correct to ban books. He was not arbitrary. And he always explained his reasons to the leadership. It was difficult enough to absorb, discipline, and train the dozens of youngsters who straggled in each week from Los Angeles and San Francisco. They had to be cut off, temporarily, from the distracting influences of family and mass media, so their minds were free to accept socialism now—the giving life.

"Once we have them wagging their tails behind them . . ."

Jeanie objected to that phrase, and she told Eli so.

"They're happy. If they're wagging their tails behind them, they're happy," Eli insisted. "Ask them."

And they seemed happy enough, and Jeanie, walking slowly back to her cabin to roll a cigarette from the can of Bugler tobacco and light a Bengali Lime Spiritual Sky incense stick and planning to ask Dennis for a little something to lighten her mood, deduced from her lack of rage and restlessness that she was happy too.

She was happy that the breeze had stopped and the whirring stopped and it was silent. Her face broke through the surface of the lake into the damp silence. She lay as still as she could, waiting for all the motion in her to stop.

It sounded like a door opening. It was the first signal she had that she was indoors, rather than out on the shore of an ocean. He was touching her shoulders and shaking her gently. She looked at the fingers on her shoulder. They were flat fingers, like Popsicle sticks, with manicured nails, fingers she'd recognize anywhere.

"Wake up, Jeanette. I need you now."

Her eyelids fluttered, closed, fluttered, focusing on and off the flat fingers and the deep voice with its endearing rust around the edges. She felt close to him. She considered opening her eyes fully and turning her head and taking in the full blazing furnace of his face and wild beard. She loved him almost too much to look at him. She might be consumed. And what was wrong with consumed? She had nothing to do with her own life, why not let it be consumed in ecstasy?

He lifted her into a sitting position. Her eyes kept opening and closing. He brushed the stray red hairs from her cheeks.

She smiled at him with her eyes closed, a soft pliant smile, her face veiled with secret memories.

"I need you now, Jeanette." Eli stood up suddenly, which startled her into opening her eyes. She saw a panoramic view of blue sky and white clouds in his face. She saw him walk away from her and open the door. "Can you prop this open, Dennis? It's stuffy in here."

Apparently the answer was no, because Eli closed the door again. "Let's go for a walk," she said suddenly, her fat tongue making the words slur.

"What did you say?"

"Walk."

He helped her up and she walked stumblingly across the small room, gazing at the wall as if it were a field of muddy, rocky, hilly land.

"Jeanette. Will you help? I believe the same things you believe."

She turned to gaze at him, nodding with unnatural vigor.

"We have worlds to remake—mountains to move. I need you."

She kept nodding and her lips moved over and over until at last he heard her faint words. "Your wish is my command." They felt like milk on her tongue. He helped her sit down on the white couch. She smiled. "Your wish is my dish."

He laughed, his heart full of the gentle humor of that old old joke they'd shared, and she laughed too, pleased as always to see the laughter roaring from behind his beard and to feel so intimate with the great godhead.

She leaned her head casually on his shoulder. "The landlord is watching us."

He didn't understand. She motioned through the thick mirror where she thought she saw the shape of Dennis's glasses. His head appeared at the door. They heard the high-pitched scream which seemed to come from very far away.

Then Eli stood up and let her slide down on the couch by herself. Then he ran after Dennis, leaving the door open. Then Dennis's head appeared again and the door slammed shut.

19

Thomas was in a great state of frustration even before the lights went out. He didn't understand why the phones kept ringing even though they were off the hook, why the lights flickered, flickered, then went off completely. He imagined that the forces of chaos were closing in; that peace and harmony were losing ground. He had been on outside assignment for two days and nights, and now that he was inside he had no chance at the meditation room, the good fellowship at mealtimes, the blissful free hours he had known on Vancouver. When he mentioned that he needed a break to Dennis Blastrom, who kept darting in and out of his private closet at the end of the hall where, it seems, things of great importance were going on, Dennis just shrugged him off. Thomas's needs were not being met. If his needs were not met in the Church of All he'd rather go outside and get a beer and pizza. Then the lights went out and he had to stand in the dark without even his needlepoint to console him.

After several minutes in the dark, Thomas sat back down in his chair and picked up his needlepoint. He held a flashlight under one arm, struggling to keep the beam of light on his work. He couldn't quite manage it. So he tried holding the flashlight between his knees with the beam directed upward. That worked better, though it was uncomfortable. It was then that he realized that he was almost out of thread. The kit had left him short again. He had only a few inches of background left, but as he carefully measured the remaining strands against the canvas, he would definitely be short.

When Helena Carpenter came bobbing down the hall, swinging a lantern and humming a chant, Thomas was bent over the canvas, measuring again. She began to giggle. He was as large as a fullback and looked quite absurd with his knees pinched together to hold up the flashlight and his hands clutching the canvas. He dropped the canvas and glared at her. "Tell me where Faye is."

"Oh, who knows, darling. It's crazy downstairs."

The flashlight slipped and the light shone on Thomas's groin. Helena was delighted at this and put down her lantern so that its red glow lit the area under her thin cotton skirt. She smiled, waiting to be hugged, petted, and kissed by this big football player of a man who pretended he didn't like her.

He stood up suddenly and the flashlight landed on the soft rug, but didn't go out. "You know where Faye is. I have to see her."

"I know where I am," Helena said, her thin legs and panties illuminated by the lantern's red glow. She raised her arms awkwardly, touching the tuft of her hair. She said something else, leaning toward him until he could see her aquamarine eyes glowing in the darkness.

There was a roar in his ears. He kicked over the lantern, which went out. He grabbed the front of her shirt with one hand and began to methodically smash her against the wall. He held her easily, as if she were a kitten. Her head snapped back loosely each time her spine hit the wall. Her scream was very high-pitched. There was blood running from her nose and the corner of her mouth. Her shirt was pulled way down in front so that her small breasts peeked out.

When Eli Zinger and Dennis ran out into the hall they

didn't know whether Thomas was trying to kill her or rape her. Dennis threw his body on Thomas's arm with a yell. Thomas gave her one more smash against the wall, then released her and she sank to the floor.

"She started it," Thomas said to Eli. "I would never start up with her, but she started it. She wouldn't tell me where Faye is."

Helena sniffled on the floor. "I did not start it."

Dennis picked up the flashlight and shone it on Helena.

"Over here," Eli said. Dennis directed the light so that Eli could unhook the walkie-talkie that hung on the back of Thomas's chair. Eli called Joseph Cordite and demanded a medical team. Cordite's voice crackled over the walkie-talkie in angry assertion that he had his hands full already. "This is an emergency," Eli said quietly.

Cordite replied that he had a dozen emergencies at the moment.

Eli put the walkie-talkie near Helena's mouth. "Give him a scream, dear." A high-pitched wail came out of her body. "It's the Senator's daughter," Eli said.

"Oh shit," Cordite's voice crackled. "I'll be right there."

Eli knelt near Helena, touching her white baby hair. "Can you move?"

She couldn't, not even enough to shake her head, and tears ran down her face.

Eli spoke to her in hushed, deep tones, chanting, smiling, bestowing his presence on her as a balm. Dennis relit her lantern. Thomas Baker leaned against the wall, breathing hard, waiting for his turn to speak.

They heard Cordite talking to someone down the corridor, chiding the repairmen for not getting the telephones back in order yet. He came lurching toward them with his flashlight swinging, leading two Allees who carried a stretcher. It was a slow, painful process, lifting Helena onto the stretcher, and they all thought silently that her back was broken. She screamed for Eli to come with her, but Cordite held on to his arm, shaking his head. "I'll send him down to you in a minute, Helena. I need to speak to him first."

Cordite pulled Eli away from Thomas and Dennis. "You must go down to the lobby. There's chaos down there. The damn lights are off, the telephones are ringing, the repairmen are wandering around like they don't know what they're doing, all your little followers are chanting in the corners looking helpless, and to top it all off there's some kind of a demonstration outside the hotel. The police captain came in to warn me it may get violent."

Eli smiled, touching Cordite briefly on the shoulder. "I'll see what I can do."

"What are we going to do about Helena Carpenter?"

"Accidents happen when the lights go out."

There was a pause. "I have only one more inch of the background left and I'm out of thread," Thomas said. "The kit is supposed to have enough! I know I didn't lose any of it. Will someone please tell me where I can find her godship Faye? She'll help me get some. Oh, it's so hard to match white exactly."

"You're going to have to lock him up," Eli said very softly to Cordite.

"That's really tough. Of all days, I need him today."

"Take him into one of the sleeping rooms. Have Dennis give him something."

Cordite turned to Dennis for the first time. He was standing on the threshold of his control room, his eyes darting from light to light. "What made you ask that your little daughter be brought up here?"

Dennis stared at him without comprehension.

"I would think the nursery would be the best place for her in all this confusion."

"I never . . . I didn't send for her. She isn't here."

"What the fuck is going on!" Cordite roared.

Eli touched each of them on the arm and sent them to various tasks. "It's a day of chaos. We'll get through it."

"What do you want me to do with Jeanette?" Dennis asked.

"Just keep her on ice until I get back."

20

When the phones started ringing Leelannee knew it was her mother calling. She sat with the other children of All at a big round table, staring at her brown rice and seaweed. A lady asked her if she wanted soy sauce. She answered, "Yes, I mean no." The lady splashed some over her rice and kept moving around the table, paying no attention to the phone that was ringing behind a door somewhere. A foot kicked Leelannee under the table. She thought it was that boy with the shaved head and a mean smile. She touched the rice with her spoon, trying to separate it from the squiggly green things. The phone kept right on ringing. Finally, Leelannee got down from her chair and approached the lady, who was gulping down her food at another round table filled with big people wearing gold discs. Nobody was talking. The only noise was the phones ringing. Leelannee pulled on the lady's arm until she bent an ear. "I want to talk to my mother," she said, "she's calling me."

The lady put her arm around Leelannee and pulled her so close she could hardly breathe. "That's not your mother, your godship. There's something wrong with the phone. It's just some troublemakers."

"My mother is a troublemaker," Leelannee grinned. Paul always called her that. So, did you make any trouble for the system today, Jeanie?

The lady laughed and a few others did. "She's harmonizing very well, don't you think?"

"God willing."

"Go eat now, darling."

Leelannee started for her table but she moved off in the wrong direction in the vast dining hall. She walked past several tables, realized she was far from the other children, and thought she might as well find the telephone and talk to the troublemakers. No one stopped her. She walked very very quietly along the wooden floors, looking down at her feet. At the far end of the room a door swung open and more people filed in with trays in their hands. Leelannee went out under their elbows.

In the hall there was a telephone with the receiver off the hook. It was ringing. Leelannee picked up the receiver but all she heard was ringing. She opened her mouth very wide and began to wail.

When the lights went out Leelannee was back in the nursery. "As long as the lights are out, we might as well go to sleep," the lady said, lighting candles and sticking them in saucers.

Leelannee had never seen a candle before, except briefly on birthday cakes, and she lay on her cot sucking her thumb and staring at the quivering light. She was just falling asleep when they told her to get up. The lady was standing over her, shaking her, pulling her thumb out of her mouth. "Get up now, your godship. Your father is asking for you."

Leelannee tried to hold on to her sleep. She let the woman

pull her upright, but slumped down again as soon as she let go. She started to cry loudly, which woke her up completely, and she twisted to make it harder for the lady to pull the shirt over her head. She kept crying, as loud as she could, watching the other children wake up in the candlelight, struggling to kick off her shoes as soon as the lady put them on. She didn't stop crying, in fact, until the woman led her to the nursery door and turned her over to another woman who was carrying a light that glowed red. Leelannee glanced up at the woman with the lantern and closed her mouth to stop the crying. The woman was Gail Macellaney, who took her by the hand and led her down the dark corridor.

"I had a night-dream," Leelannee told Gail.

"This whole thing is a nightmare," Gail said in an undertone.

"I want to see Mommy."

"And Mommy wants to see you, honey. Soon as we get out of here, we're gonna see . . ."

Gail pulled her into a staircase. It was very dark, and the red lantern made shadows hover over the bannister. Leelannee planted her feet firmly, grabbed on to the top of the bannister, and refused to move. She could hear a telephone ringing faintly in the distance. She wanted to talk to her mother. Gail's face looked intensely ghoulish in the red light. Her head was tall and pointed on the shadow above the bannister. Leelannee opened her mouth and began to wail.

Gail set the lantern down and sat on the top step. She took Leelannee on her lap, pressing her close, rocking her and talking quietly but rapidly. "I'm going to take you to your mommy, honey. Your mommy asked me to come and get you. We're going to walk down these stairs, five flights of stairs, down to the basement and right out the door and then we'll be outside and we'll get in a car and we'll go and see your mommy."

Leelannee put her face between the bulges of Gail's breasts. "Gail, when we get outside . . ."

"Yeah?"

"Is it gonna be nighttime?"

"Yeah. It's nighttime, honey. It'll be all right. You'll fall asleep in the taxi and when you wake up you'll see your mommy. And she'll be so glad to see you. She's all worried about you."

"Where is she?"

"She's—she's waiting for you at my house."

"Are you a bad guy? Dennis said you're a bad guy."

Gail held her close, putting on her funny voice. "Me, a bad guy? That's the weirdest thing I ever heard. I never been so insulted in my life." She lifted Leelannee to her feet. "I can't carry you, kid, because I got the lantern. Just hold on tight to the bannister and go down one step at a time. Are you big enough to do it?"

"I'm big."

They walked slowly down the flights of stairs without talking. They could hear telephones ringing at each landing and voices calling. Leelannee got into the rhythm of the descent and was as surprised as Gail Macellaney when after four flights the staircase ended.

"Oh shit, I picked the wrong staircase," Gail muttered.

"I don't want to go up again," Leelannee said.

"No, we won't, we'll just have to risk it." She opened the heavy fire door slowly and stuck her head and her lantern out. It took a few minutes until she realized she was in the main lobby. Lantern and candles were placed far apart, flickering like campfires on a vast dark battlefield. The cops had flashlights with strong beams. Clusters of Allees gathered around various lanterns joining arms and swaying to chants. But there were other Allees, with taller and bigger frames, who stood at the front doors, obviously on guard.

Gail closed the door and sat on the bottom step near Leelannee. She unfolded a Xeroxed sketch of the floor plan of the Reverence Hotel and tried to pinpoint her location. According to all her calculations the staircase she had chosen should have led to the basement. She tried to see her error, but for several moments her eyes repeated her mistake over and over. Then it hit her that perhaps the staircase to the basement adjoined this one and if she stepped out in the lobby she would see another door. Leelannee was leaning on her knee now, her eyes glazed with sleep. She would have liked to carry the child, but was afraid of stumbling and being discovered.

"You know, Leelannee, I don't really believe in material incentives, but, if you can keep quiet for the next few minutes until I tell you you can talk again, I'll buy any any damn toy you want."

"I want a Boopsy doll," Leelannee said immediately.

"You have a Boopsy doll."

"I lost her head."

"Oh, okay, be quiet and you'll get a new doll."

"Can you buy just a new head?"

"I don't think so. Okay. Quiet now, here goes." She opened the door and strode out shining her lantern on the adjoining walls. She saw what she thought was another stairwell door about fifteen feet away, but between them and the door stood a middle-aged man who was hitching up his pants as he spoke into a walkie-talkie. Near him stood two Allee guards and a police captain. The staircase door had closed behind Gail. She kept Leelannee close to her right side, and kept her light almost at shoulder level so it didn't illuminate the child. She stayed near the wall, uncertain about what would happen if she entered the vast battlefield of flickering lights. They made it past the knot of men without being noticed. Gail heard them talking about the demonstration and smiled to herself, already writing her account of the incident for the *Mirrormart Worker*. Freeing our sister and her child from the clutches of the unethical guru Eli Zinger. . . . With demonstrators on the outside, and some very involved telephone repairmen on the inside, the workers' coalition was successful in freeing our sister and her child. . . .

She reached the door and tried it with held breath. It opened and it was indeed a staircase going down. She pulled Leelannee inside and leaned on the door for a moment, breathing hard.

"Can I talk now? Do I get a Boopsy doll?"

"Shhh, not yet, not until we're outside."

"It's going to be nighttime?"

"Shhh."

The steps were narrower here, and led, precisely as Gail expected, into the basement kitchen, which from her first cautious raising of the lantern appeared to be large and empty. Then the lights went on.

After a moment of blindness, Gail realized there were other people in the kitchen. She turned the knob on her lantern until it went out. The row of women at the stoves blew out their candles and smiled at each other. Gail noticed a door near her, opened it, and pulled Leelannee into the dark, roomy pantry. She held her hand over Leelannee's mouth as the child began to speak. "Go to sleep now, Lee." She sat on the floor and put the child's head on her lap.

21

Jeanie waited a long time for Eli Zinger to come back. She'd had a sweet moment of connectedness. She tried not to drift away from it. But the air she was breathing was stale and her head ached from the sound of the door slamming shut. She heard doors slamming farther and farther away down long corridors. The sounds echoed significantly in her brain, until she began to search for symbolic meaning. What was the door slamming shut on? Slam the door on the old world and enter the new. But this couldn't be the new world. The air was too static. And the room was too small, even to a person stretched out on a couch. It was the smallest damn room. Its four corners pinched together and the walls seemed to slant to a point above her head, though they never quite peaked. That was symbolic too. Nothing peaked any more. You can't get a new high out of an old drug, Dennis said one time. She needed a couple of old aspirins. He didn't have to *slam* the door. When she left she shut it as quietly as she could.

Why was she so seasick? Was this the two-dollar stateroom she took on the ferry from Vancouver Island? Leelannee had an aversion to large rooms and crowds. Leelannee was just a baby so she won. But Jeanie hated to be cramped in a tiny room on a moving boat. The ferry moved smoothly, slowly, but she could feel the vibrations of the engine and the small stateroom did not feel stable. But where was Leelannee? She tried to rise from the couch but fell back, over and over, her stomach churning with nausea as if fat white-capped waves were smashing against her sides. She assured herself that Leelannee was sleeping in the corner sucking her thumb.

It was her fault. She didn't have to take the seasick ferry. She could have flown off the island in Cordite's private plane. That was quite beside the point. If she wanted to lean on Joseph Cordite she might as well stay and join the newly consecrated Church of All. No, she wanted to go back to New York where the only chicken she had to look at was neatly quartered and wrapped in cellophane. Where the thousands of stoned California youths who were flocking to Eli Zinger to be found would just be a sixty-second news spot.

Jeanie kept her eyes on the emergency exit. She kept reading the sign that said: ALL PASSENGERS ARE REQUIRED TO PUT ON LIFEBELTS AND GO TO THEIR MUSTER STATIONS WHENEVER GENERAL ALARM BELLS RING. She liked the tone of the sign. Muster stations, general alarm. Man the muster stations! Leelannee was asleep on the bench in the corner, wrapped in a red flannel blanket. She hadn't been sure until the moment she stepped on the ferry that Zinger would actually permit them to leave. Others had been denied permission. But she was senior leadership; she had the right to a two-week visit to her parents; and she had made sure to confide her real plans to no one. So it was goodbye to Port Alice, Port McNeill, Kelsey Bay, Campbell River. She would never be back to Port Alice. She was disconnected.

She ached at the spot where she had disconnected. Alone, adrift with a child, it was not romantic, it did not appeal to her, it was a two-dollar stateroom that made her nauseous, and a plane ticket paid for by her parents. She would never again look out in the ocean and know Japan was the first land point west of the commune. She would miss it raining every day all winter—weather so incredibly green and wet that it had a fairy tale aura, especially when she was freshly stoned. Pebbles, driftwood, waterfalls on Blind River. She knew what she wanted to remember. Oh, then I spent two years digging oysters and clams at low tide and staining my fingers with blackberries as I popped them into Leelannee's mouth. It wasn't all bad. But I got tired of it. You know, the war in Vietnam finally ended, which made it a *little* easier to come back to the city. And then Eli Zinger got this Church idea in his head and I couldn't shake him out of it.

She would forget the darker side. She had stolen documents in her knapsack. She would put them in her parents' safe deposit box in case Dennis Blastrom or Eli Zinger or Joseph Cordite ever showed up to bother her. Otherwise they could crumble to dust. She wanted to forget the darker side.

She left Leelannee in the stateroom asleep and went on deck. She saw a seagull flying backward. The mainland of British Columbia was ahead of her and she anticipated dragging around baggage and baby, getting to the airport, dealing on the airplane with the first straight people she'd seen in two years, dealing with her parents. She was good at forgetting. When Dennis called her down for skipping meditation room for a week, she told him she was in such a high state she just forgot to go. And when she was depressed she'd walk out in the woods and think instead of asking Dennis for a little something to lighten her mood. And she rocked and sang Leelannee to sleep each night so Dennis wouldn't put anything in her milk to stop her from crying.

But she ached at the spot where she was disconnected. She had so wanted to be part of something, something grand and radical and worthwhile. Oh, that was when I was much younger, she'd explain to the new friends in New York. I didn't know what it was all about, so I got involved with Zinger—yes, he *is* a very special person, but then so am I.

Seagulls shrieked and circled near the shore. She wanted to wait until the last possible moment to wake Leelannee. She opened the door to the stateroom but she didn't see the child. Her heart slammed in fear. She ran in and found she'd rolled off the bench and was sleeping on the floor, still wrapped in her blanket.

Jeanie hoisted herself up on the couch and looked carefully in all the corners of the room, even though it made her seasick when she turned her head. She didn't see Leelannee. The whirring sound started up again. This was some kind of meditation room. It made her remember certain lovely moments. Of course there were lovely moments, moments when she was soaringly happy and impatient that the world had problems. Moments when she could be happy even though the U.S. was bombing dikes in North Vietnam where the peasants pinned letters on each other's backs so they could learn to read as they tilled the land. Lovely moments. She glanced at the vents near the floor and tried to read them as if they were a sign saying all passengers go to their muster stations whenever general alarm bells ring. Where was her muster station? She saw a shadow on the other side of the mirror. "Leave me the fuck alone!" she screamed out, and her words bounced back at her from the corners of the room. She lunged toward the mirror, but swooned to the floor before she reached it. Before she lost consciousness she could have sworn she heard Paul's voice.

22

Dennis led Thomas Baker into the spare room he used for sleeping when he was involved in all-night experiments. He gave Thomas two white sleeping pills and told him to lie down and rest. He drew a glass of water from the hotel sink and handed it to him, musing about keeping Jeanette "on ice" for Eli, and whether or not that meant he should renew the dose of pectamine and dimethyl sulfoxide. He didn't notice that Thomas pushed the pills into his cheek with his tongue and swallowed only the water. Thomas lay down on the bed without taking his shoes off.

"What happened to you?" Dennis asked, almost without interest.

"She started it." Thomas folded his hands behind his bald head and shut his eyes. The pills in the corner of his mouth began to dissolve in a bitter taste. It was dark in the room except for the light of Dennis's flashlight. "Leave me a candle," Thomas said.

"I don't have one on me. I'll be back in a second." Dennis left the room, carefully locking the door. He hurried down the corridor to his control room. As he was unlocking the door he heard footsteps and whirled around to find two men had come up behind him in the dark. He opened the door a bit so that the light produced by the emergency generator shone on them. They were wearing dark green telephone company uniforms with gadgets hanging off their belts.

"We need to check your phone," the Spanish one said, pointing into the control room.

"I haven't got a telephone in there."

"Well, you got a light on, and that's better than the rest of this hotel. Man, have you been down to the other floors? It's crazy down there. People running around. How come you got lights on?"

Dennis stepped into the room, starting to close the door.

Paul held a piece of spliced wire close to Dennis's glasses. "We gotta check the wires in there."

Dennis peered at the wire, wondering.

"Here, take it," Paul said, pushing the wire into his hand

and at the same time pushing Dennis into the control room. Justino followed, closing the door.

They stared through the mirror at Jeanie, who was slumped on the floor in front of the couch. Her tea-colored hair was frizzed around her face. Her skin had a polished ivory sheen. Paul wasn't sure she was alive.

In the second's pause Dennis lunged toward his desk. He pushed the button on the humidifier that sent the pectamine mixture into the meditation room again. He also pushed the button under the table that sealed the room with a hissing sound.

Paul pulled a heavy wrench off his tool belt and hit Dennis full force on the back of his neck. Dennis fell toward the mirror, which shook from the impact. Paul pushed Dennis to the floor and picked up a chair, about to try to smash the mirror.

"Hold it man. She's gonna get cut."

Justino pushed a button and tried the door to the meditation room, but the heavy handle held fast. The humidifier hummed at high speed.

Paul waited with chair aloft as Justino tried another button. "Come on. We gotta do this quick." He heard his voice being picked up by the open microphone and spoke into it.

"Jeanie. This is Paul. You gotta get up, honey. We're gonna get you out of there."

They watched her struggle and fail to rise.

"Compañera, this is Justino. Try to roll. That's it, just roll over, away from the glass. Good. Keep rolling, good, one more time, that's it, go right under the couch." As he spoke Justino's fingers ran under the table and found the release button for the door. They heard it unseal with a hiss.

Paul pulled it open and ran to drag Jeanie out from under the couch. The air in the chamber made him dizzy so he tried to work fast. Jeanie had rolled way under the couch. She was dead weight in his arms. He tried to get her out without bruising her skin which looked so damp and fragile. She looked half drowned. By the time he'd lifted her up he felt a seasick motion in his stomach and had to caution himself not to sit down on the couch to rest. A few moments later they were out in the corridor, trying to get Jeanie to walk between them, but her legs dragged.

The hallway was dark, and they shut the door to the control room so that its light wouldn't reveal them. They used only the pen flashlight which hung from Justino's belt. Paul was talking gently to Jeanie, begging her to walk, to wake up, to say something.

They heard a loud pounding from one of the rooms on the corridor. A man was shouting that he had to get out, that someone should open the door. He sounded desperate and full of anger. Justino stopped near the door, his white teeth smiling against puff lips. "Maybe we should free all their prisoners."

Paul propped Jeanie up against the wall, tapping her face. "We have to get her to walk."

"I think we left too quickly. We should have searched the guy we knocked out for keys."

"Something smelled funny in that room," Paul said. "Maybe if she sits here for a few minutes she'll be able to walk. We'll never get away with carrying her out."

"Okay, who's going back?"

There was loud kicking coming from the door near them. The bellowing got louder.

"You think I'm going to leave you alone with her?" Paul asked.

"Hey."

"Just joking. You go back if you want. But be quick, this spot is so exposed."

"Don't turn on any lights."

Paul let Jeanie sink to the floor, rolled her onto her stomach and began to give artificial respiration. After three pushes she began to groan. "I'm going to throw up." He relented, talking to her constantly in a soothing voice, but that was all she said in the three or four minutes it took Justino to return to the control room, take the keys out of Dennis's pocket and, as an afterthought while he was pushing the off button on the humidifier, snatch up the papers that lay near the typewriter.

The corridor was so dark that Paul didn't see Justino until his white teeth flashed in a smile at the sight of Jeanie sitting up. "Great, now can she walk?"

"Can we give her just a few more minutes?"

Justino shone his penlight on his watch. "I hope Gail got the baby out. I don't want to spend time here. Someone could come any minute."

The pounding on the door near them started up again at the sound of their voices. Justino stepped quietly near the door and listened to Thomas calling for a candle, for white thread, for a chance to speak to Faye. He tried several keys in the lock until he found one that fit, and the prisoner bellowed even louder at the sound of the key. But Justino hesitated a moment and stepped back to Paul.

"You think I should let him out? He sounds weird."

"They all get weird in this place."

"Pull Jeanie back a little bit, out of the way. I think I'm going to let him out."

Justino opened the door with his key and stood back as Thomas Baker hurled himself into the dark hallway, stumbling about until he found Justino and touched his shoulders.

"Telephone company," Justino said. "You gotta phone in there?"

Thomas nodded heavily. "Where's Faye Zinger? You see

her? They never give you enough thread in kits, I should know better than to buy kits, but Faye always manages to get me some more thread."

Justino touched the corners of his mustache, nodding with pursed lips. "You need thread, eh?"

"Where is she? Did you see Faye?"

"I think I did. I think that was the young lady I saw heading down to the basement."

"The basement?"

Thomas turned, and began to run down the hall.

"Hey, man," Justino called. "Which of those elevators goes to the basement?"

"The middle one," Thomas called back, disappearing into the darkness.

Justino returned to Paul and Jeanie, who was still sitting on the floor, despite Paul's efforts. "Shit, what'd ya send him to the basement for?" Paul asked.

"I like to add to the confusion. That guy must be one of their mistakes." Justino kneeled in front of Jeanie. He held on to her hands. "Get the hell up!" he said in a sharp, but hushed tone. Jeanie made an immediate attempt to stand, and Justino helped her. "Now walk, one foot in front of the other, walk straight! You look like you're sick. Walk straight. I don't want anyone to notice you. Walk straight and you'll walk right out of here!"

Jeanie responded obediently to his commands. With Paul's arm firmly around her waist she seemed to be walking normally enough. Paul started for the staircase, but Justino shook his head. "She'll never make twenty-one flights. I say we take the center elevator, as soon as it comes back up."

"We decided on the stairs," Paul protested.

"I didn't know she'd be in this condition. What the hell did they do to her? You know when I went back to the control room there was some kind of wet gas all over the place. I turned it off. I didn't want to kill that guy you hit."

"Was he still out?"

"He's taking a long siesta. Don't worry, he's okay. I didn't see any blood. He's breathing."

"I think that was Leelannee's father," Paul said, leaning against the wall with Jeanie waiting for the elevator. "Hey, Justino, you really think this elevator's gonna come? The electricity's out!"

Justino snorted, and they had walked almost to the stairwell when the overhead lights suddenly came on. They were too startled to say anything, glancing around the miraculously vacant corridor. Jeanie's head drooped as she walked, and in full light there was no mistaking that she was not well or fully conscious. "The elevator again!" Justino said, running ahead to ring for it, listening with his ear to the door as the grinding sound started. It came in less than a minute and indeed had a basement button.

Justino sat down at the brass operator's stool and opened the panel, which had a broken lock. While Paul held the door to keep the elevator from responding to calls from other floors, Justino fiddled with the large ring of keys on his belt until he found one that fit the hole that turned the elevator onto manual control. Orange lights on the panel lit up from many floors, but Justino sent it express to the basement, while Paul and Jeanie leaned back clutching the railing. Paul's face drained white from the rapid descent and Justino laughed as he saw him. "Don't worry, my papa's been an elevator operator for thirty-three years. He works at the Forty-second Street library; you ever been there?"

Paul shook his head, trying to listen and allow himself to be distracted from his desire to faint.

"They put in automatic elevators there years ago, but the

union made them keep the operators on until they're old enough to retire. It's really crazy, they stand there in these maroon uniforms with white gloves and operate an elevator that could run just as good without them. Of course my mama wouldn't run too good without my papa's checks."

They seemed literally to hit the ground floor and the elevator bucked up and down a few times. Justino opened the brass doors cautiously. The cement walled area was vacant, but he could hear a commotion of some kind in the adjoining room, which they supposed was the kitchen.

"Walk, gringa!" She responded to the command, but her head hung down as she walked and her face was smeared with confusion.

Thomas Baker had reached the kitchen area panting from galloping down twenty-two flights of stairs. His face was bright red, right over the scalp of his bald head. He raced into the kitchen shouting, "Where is Faye? I have to find her."

"Take it easy, Thomas," said one of the two Allees who had been assigned to guard the back door to the hotel.

Thomas waved his needlepoint canvas in their faces, then ran to show it to the three girls who were doing the kitchen work. "I need more white thread. She got me some last time. She's a merciful lady."

"She hasn't been here," one of the girls said. "A lot's been going on today, you have to be a little patient."

"Patient!" Thomas lunged for her, but she stepped out of the way quickly and instead he pulled open the handle of the huge refrigerator. He grabbed a large open carton of eggs and threw them on the floor. The guards reached for him, but he swept them out of the way with his powerful arms and began to throw the whole contents of the refrigerator on the floor. There was a smash of maple syrup and carrot juice and a vat of brown rice landed on the sandaled feet of the guards. Then Thomas reared suddenly and ran from the room. The guards took after him in a fury. The three girls shook their heads and went into the bathroom to wash away the maple syrup that had splashed on their legs.

The bottoms of their shoes were sticky with syrup as Paul and Justino led Jeanie through the kitchen to the hotel service entrance. They were just a few feet away when they heard a door open behind them. Paul pulled the wrench off his tool belt and whirled around, letting Jeanie fall onto Justino for support. He waited a few seconds, listening for the footsteps, then saw Gail walking toward him, holding the child's hand.

"What the . . ." Paul exclaimed.

"I got trapped," Gail whispered. "Let's go!"

"Shhhhhh!" said Leelannee.

The night was quite cold. Neither Jeanie nor Leelannee had jackets, but they breathed the icy air with pleasure. Paul hurried them up the ramp to the sidewalk, trying to keep in the shadows along the edges. Across the street a taxi was parked in a no parking zone. The driver had his feet up on the dashboard and his hat pulled over his eyes, but he straightened up instantly when Gail's face appeared at the window and opened the door.

They could hear the demonstration of about fifty people which massed on the side of the Reverence Hotel. Antagonistic shouts flew into the wind like discarded newspapers.

"Well," said Gail, as she settled in the front seat with Leelannee on her lap, "what's been going on out here?"

The driver shook his head. "I wouldn't have missed it for the world. Let's see. There was an ambulance and the rumor is that the Senator's daughter got killed by some maniac. Then when the coalition decided you guys were in there too long they rushed the front entrance and kept the cops busy for a while."

"Anyone arrested?"

"Three, I heard."

"Too bad," Gail said.

"Did it have any effect on the inside?"

"I don't know."

Leelannee had turned in the seat and was gazing through the plastic partition at her mother. Jeanie's head was leaning against Paul's shoulder and her eyes were open, but unseeing. "You said Mommy was at home," the child accused Gail.

"I made a mistake."

"What's the matter with her?"

"She's tired. She'll be better once we get her home."

"I want to sit back there."

"No, honey, let Paul and Justino take care of her. You stay here with me."

But Leelannee had begun to kick and scramble with such energy that at last Gail asked the driver to pull over and let Leelannee go to the back seat.

They all watched anxiously as Leelannee climbed onto Jeanie's lap and tried to push herself into an embrace. Jeanie's arms lay limply at her sides, and the child wiggled frantically, hugging her neck, and trying to fit her face against her mother's chest. When the cab started again Leelannee began to slide forward, and Jeanie's arms went up to stop her fall. The child seemed satisfied by this and climbed into Paul's extended arms.

The driver was the first to break the silence. "Where to?"

Gail checked her watch, snorting. "She could be on the Eddie Market show in two hours if we could only wake her up. Let's go to the loft and have a stab at it."

"I'm going to take her home," Paul said. "And if she doesn't snap out of it by tomorrow I'm going to take her to the hospital."

Jeanie's lips fluttered. She said something they didn't understand. Paul put his arm around her, holding her head against his shoulder. He had Leelannee on the other knee. Jeanie noticed that he was acting very concerned about her. She wondered who he was. He was comfortable to lean against in the tossing car. The little girl was leaning against him too. Jeanie moved her hand until she touched his ear. "I want to walk."

The cab pulled up at the loft building. Gail asked her to come upstairs, but Jeanie shook her head no. The dark buildings of the industrial area swayed as she shook her head. Paul tried to pull her toward his battered white convertible which had collected two tickets since this morning.

"No," she said quite distinctly, "I have a headache. I better walk."

Gail peeled off her blue parka and gave it to Jeanie. Then she hurried Justino and Leelannee into the cafeteria on the corner of Seventh Avenue. Paul tried to urge Jeanie to follow them, but she balked, refusing to enter any doorways.

23

They had forced her to walk down a dark corridor, driven her in a squealing taxi, shoved her into an oversized jacket, and now they wanted her to step over another strange threshold. She wasn't going to do it. She didn't want another door slamming shut behind her. She held her head up as high as she could and kept her eyes open, though they longed to close and keep out the careening city. Pieces of broken glass pressed into her shoes as she walked the deserted streets of the warehouse district. Garbage bags huddled near the curb. Cars, taxis. She was back in New York. Her stomach settled. Her arms swung stiffly in the unfamiliar jacket. If she put questions to herself spikes of light went off in her head. She had to stay calm. She had to be ready when Eli Zinger came back for her. She knew he would come for her, sometime. She was surprised that he let the ferry leave Nanaimo. She clearly remembered the ferry leaving and the two-dollar stateroom with Leelannee wrapped in a red flannel blanket.

The sidewalks pressed up against the bottom of her shoes. The man walking next to her held her arm until the traffic light changed. He was trying to make conversation; he didn't know the conversation convention was canceled. She couldn't stay on the ferry forever. She was back in New York. Her face told her it was winter, night winds blowing. It wasn't supposed to be winter. She had come back to New York in the summer, she remembered that.

Summertime New York was an outrage to her Vancouver vision! It was so much more crumbled, faded, crowded, and littered than when she left. The men wore undershirts in the street and the older women didn't cover their bumpy legs with stockings.

It was winter now, with a night wind blowing in her face and the icy sidewalks. She was going to walk until the slices of time pressed together. The walking was good. It settled her stomach and she held her head as high as she could. She had to stay calm.

She came back to New York in the summertime and wondered why she chose this transistor radio land over the chanting, suntanned youths at the Vancouver Farm. She couldn't go back but she couldn't see her way forward. She left Leelannee with her mother for a day and decided to wander up Fifth Avenue, which was less distressing to her country sensibility. As she walked she examined the sidewalk-bound trees and listened for birds.

The man walking next to her kept asking her things. He

told her to wait while he made a call from a phone booth and when she wandered off he ran after her, pulled her back to the phone booth, and held her arm as he spoke.

She closed her eyes and returned to a summer afternoon. She wanted to buy sunglasses to keep the soot out of her eyes. She wanted to walk as if she were a person who inspired great fear, who was something to contend with. She'd walked two miles before she rested on the steps of the Forty-second Street library, feeling very raw at the spot where she was disconnected. She was no longer married. She was no longer Eli Zinger's political officer. She was a tourist sitting next to the lion on the steps of the Forty-second Street library.

Gail Macellaney saw her first, squealing, "Jeanie Burger! I haven't seen you since Ban the Bomb!" And it seemed such a comic thing to say that Jeanie screamed hello and they reeled in each other's arms as if they were still sixteen-year-olds defying the dean together, wearing black armbands during air raid drills and singing Pete Seeger songs in the lunchroom.

They sat on the library steps, hugging their knees, bubbling with questions. Jeanie tried out her practiced speech. "Oh, I've done a lot of things since high school. Got married, getting divorced, have a kid, spent some years on the All commune—you know, the one that's called the Church of All now—but I got tired of that. . . ."

Gail's eyebrows peaked. "I bet you did."

"Don't go for them, huh?" She waited breathlessly for Gail's reaction. Maybe she knew something Jeanie didn't.

"I think it's a reactionary group, despite their rhetoric. I mean there are probably a lot of honest people in it. But it's no accident that the youth movement is disintegrating into drugs and religious cults."

Jeanie smiled, hoping she would go on, trying not to betray the intensity of her interest. She had tried to find someone to discuss her All experiences with, but it was beyond the comprehension of most of her old friends who were married to schoolteachers and living in Westchester. "Well, if it's no accident, what is it? Some kind of a plot?"

"No, not necessarily a plot," Gail said, leaning on the stack of leaflets and newspapers she had stuffed in a plastic case. "It's just the social forces playing out their roles. I think there must be some government collusion on the drug end. They made it awfully easy for the soldiers to bring hash and heroin into the States from Vietnam and places. Maybe they figured it would cool out the antiwar movement, and in a way it did. Anyway, I'm glad you're not going back to All. There's so much meaningful work to be done in the city."

"My parents want me to go back and finish college," Jeanie said.

Gail laughed. "I finished college. I work in the meat department at Mirrormart." She whipped out a newsletter called the *Mirrormart Worker* and Jeanie skimmed through it with thrilled recognition. It was nice that the left went on prodding the working class, calling for solidarity with strikers in far-off places, announcing demonstrations around the present crisis. The familiar, crackling language drove the milky words of All from her ears.

But it was a little too familiar. "I don't know, Gail, there's something about being a third generation communist. You get burned out."

"We've got a couple of you red diaper babies in the coalition," Gail said. "You have to do *something*."

She did have to do something. She had to be connected. She couldn't stay a tourist in summertime New York sitting near the lion. . . .

Jeanie was moving her lips forcefully through this part of her reverie. Paul noticed she was attracting attention from people on the street. They were standing on Seventh Avenue, waiting for the light to change. It had gone on for too long now. She'd traced the same four blocks over and over. Paul had stopped to call her parents and they agreed to let her walk it off a while, but now his feet were cold from the icy sidewalks and her motions were getting wilder.

Jeanie crossed the street and stopped in front of a brick wall. She could feel his impatience. He would just have to wait. She would get to him in a minute. She had a little more to run through. The present was elusive. She never really settled with Eli Zinger. She really wasn't like her grandmother. She didn't have the nerve to throw the key to the marshal's truck down the sewer. Things weren't that clear.

Paul took her arm and led her firmly toward the steamy door of the cafeteria.

"Who are you?" she asked softly. "A friend of Gail's?"

He tapped her under the chin with his fist. "I'm a friend of yours."

"If you were a friend of mine," she said very slowly, "you'd take me home." Spikes of light went off in her mind from the strain of the conversation. She held her breath, wondering whether he would take it to mean his home or her home and if she had a home at all or just that raw spot where she was disconnected. He looked very kind, very concerned about her.

"Okay, I'll take you home. Let's get Leelannee."

She hesitated before the revolving doorway of the cafeteria, but he disarmed her by opening the side door and with a single quick movement lifting her over the doorstep. He hurried her to a table where Leelannee was dozing on Gail's lap, while Justino had papers spread out among the coffee cups.

"Say, you look much better now, compañera."

"Oooh, she does, come sit by me." Gail made room for her.

Jeanie tried to stay calm. The slices of time were not fitting together. She fingered her hair, which was damp and knotted. Gail walked her to the ladies' room and helped her brush it until the tea-colored waves gleamed again. Gail said little, but peered at her anxiously. "Are you okay? Do you want something to eat?"

When they returned to the table Paul was reading the documents that Justino had snatched from the Reverence Hotel. "Here it is," he said to Gail. " 'Emergence reactions have occurred in approximately twelve percent of patients. The psychological manifestations vary in severity between pleasant dreamlike states' . . . blah blah blah . . . 'the duration ordinarily lasts no more than a few hours. In a few cases, however, recurrences have taken place up to twenty-four hours post-operatively. No residual psychological effects are known to have resulted from the use of Pectaject.' So, assuming that's what he gave her, she should be all right soon."

"I called a guy we know who's a doctor—no fault of his own—" Gail put in, "and he said we should let her rest and not talk to her too much. He said she must have had it by injection, but Justino said he didn't see any needles lying around."

Jeanie sat quite erect, stirring her coffee with deliberate concentration. There was a steamy smell of cooked food in the air. The trays were piled near her head; they were brown. The Formica table was clammy to touch. The man sitting next to her draped his arm around her shoulder. They were all wearing winter clothes, though she knew quite well it was summer.

"I'm going to take her home," Paul said.

"What about Eddie Market?"

"Oh, she's in no shape to be interviewed."

"I know that. But do you think Justino and I should take these new documents over to him and tell him the story of the kidnapping and everything?"

Paul helped Jeanie out of her chair, then rounded the table to pick up the dozing Leelannee. "I don't know what you should do. Whatever you think best. I guess the more publicity we give it the less chance they'll bother her again."

Several other people from the coalition arrived at the cafeteria and joined in the clamor. Leelannee lifted her head from Paul's shoulder and demanded to walk next to her mother. She held on to Jeanie's wrist as they left the cafeteria, stopping dead in her tracks in front of the display case. "Ma! I want gum."

Paul reached in his pocket for a coin but Leelannee shook her fists at him. "No. I want Mommy to. . . ."

Jeanie was staring straight ahead at the glass door. Things weren't that clear. But one thing became clear from talking to Gail next to the lion at the Forty-second Street library. There were lots of different ways to fight the system, but joining the Church of All was not one of them. When Eli Zinger came for her she would tell him that. If she was going to wait for the tree to fruit she was going to wait here, with the sidewalks of New York pressing up against her shoes. All her lovers would be nonmystical fellows, and her friends. . . .

Leelannee opened her mouth and the scream startled even Jeanie. The child sobbed and kicked at Paul who was trying to pick her up.

Jeanie shook her head in annoyance. The lines of memories of the last hours scattered like sand. She watched the kaleidoscopic retreat. She watched a thousand fading faces with Eli's fragrant smile fading most slowly.

"What? What'd you want, Lee?"

The child closed her mouth, tears still running. "I want gum."

"Here," Paul tried to shove the piece he had just bought into her hand.

"No gum, Leelannee," Jeanie said. "Bad for your teeth."

Leelannee leaned against the glass display case. "Please, Mommy, *please*."

Jeanie tried to smile into Paul's expectant face. "I don't remember your name."

"His name is Paul," Leelannee said.

Of course, Paul! Funny that she remembered his voice before, when she was out on deck watching the seagulls. But she didn't remember where she knew him from.

"If I can't have gum, can I have a candy?"

Jeanie bent down and scooped up the child. With the small arms squeezing her neck she waited while Paul drove the car around to the entrance, since neither she nor the baby had their coats. Jeanie stroked the child's back rhythmically, ignoring her intense whispering about Dennis, and the lights being out, and Gail promising to buy her a Boopsy doll. She just stroked and stroked the child, feeling her thin back quivering beneath the cotton shirt.

A white convertible pulled up in front of the cafeteria, but it wasn't until Leelannee told her that was Paul's car that she thought to enter it. She let Leelannee fall asleep on her shoulder before she lay her gently on the back seat of the car.

"So," Paul said, his big chest rising and falling under his blue storm coat. "You know who the kid is, huh?"

"Sure."

He drove quickly over the icy streets. Jeanie leaned her head against the door, listening to the squeak of Leelannee sucking her thumb. Was Leelannee sick? She had been so worried about Leelannee, she remembered that. She felt a horrid streak of guilt. How could she forget about Leelannee? There was something wrong with her.

They were almost to the Willis Avenue bridge when she pulled herself upright and stared at the lights going by the car window. "I thought I lost Leelannee," she said haltingly, "but then I found her on the floor . . . of the stateroom. She had rolled off the bench."

Paul reached out and stroked her cheek. "It's good that you're talking again. If you want I can try to fill you in on what's happened to you."

She felt a rush of clarity. Her body felt practically normal. The spikes of light had dimmed to a flicker. She was hungry. "What happened to Leelannee?" she said, listening to the sound of her voice as if it were another person's.

Paul spoke slowly, searching for her attention. "Your husband took her. You went to the hotel to get her back. We think they must have given you some drug. Do you remember getting a shot or drinking something?"

"I don't remember any hotel." She listened with scorched attention as he described the room they found her in, the instrumentation, their bungling escape. It all sounded dimly familiar. A story she'd heard somewhere before. But it was odd to think it had happened to her. "How come there were no lights?" she asked.

"It's coming back to you. Just go easy on yourself. I'm surprised we got out at all. The best I was hoping for was that breaking their circuits would let Gail escape with Leelannee. When we found out you were on the twenty-first floor I almost gave up. But we went ahead with it. I figured if we got arrested for trespassing and made a big stink to the police about our friend being a prisoner in the Church of All, that would be good. The place was crawling with cops. As Justino said, you know you're getting old when the cops look young to you."

"You turned the lights out?"

"Oh yeah, we gave them a run for their money."

She tried to think of something to say to keep the conversation convention flowing, to cover up her anxiety about not knowing where her apartment was or why he was taking her over the bumpy Willis Avenue bridge and down Bruckner Boulevard where, miraculously, the Bruckner Expressway was all lit up and open. Hadn't she just read in the papers that the expressway wouldn't be ready for a year? Didn't they fire a commissioner over that? Maybe he was taking her to her mother's. "I can't wait to get to bed," she said. "My head's still hurting from that door slamming."

"What door?"

"When Eli Zinger ran out Brainstorm slammed the door. Did I really go in there to get Leelannee?"

"Yes."

"Because I remember that everything was very friendly with Eli Zinger. We were going to start all over again with the same beliefs and see where they led." She leaned against the door again, her mind crowded with images and disconnected thoughts. Leaning on Eli Zinger's shoulder, the door slamming, meeting Gail by the Forty-second Street library, holding Leelannee in her arms. She had to stay calm. She looked out the window and found Paul a parking spot. She carried Leelannee into bed and triple locked the apartment door. It all looked very familiar. It was only that she didn't remember Leelannee being so tall and the rug in the living room . . . she had always meant to replace the one left by the former tenant, but she didn't remember doing it.

She sat on the bed, her face flooded with changing emotions, her eyes focused inward. Paul studied the way her hair curled and her fingernails dug into her palms. She looked up suddenly. "Well, thank you very much. . . ."

"I've been sleeping with you for over a month," he said. "I'd like to stay tonight."

Jeanie smiled, then giggled at the situation. She had misplaced segments of her life. The pages were all out of order. But here, by some miracle, stood a rather good-looking and very nice guy who was taking care of her.

"I'll sleep on the couch," he said. "Don't worry about me. I'm just the bodyguard."

She nodded, undressing in the bathroom, leaving a small light on near the bed, watching him as he lay on the couch under a blanket he'd found by himself. She commanded herself to sleep. She hugged the pillow and twisted the covers tight around her feet.

"Maybe we should watch the Eddie Market show," Paul said. "Gail may be on it."

"You can watch it."

He walked across the room in his shorts and turned on the TV. She lay in bed marveling at the fact that she didn't feel seasick, that the air was crisp and dry, that Leelannee was safe in bed. She felt she had everything she had ever wanted.

24

She opened her eyes slowly, hoping that when the darkness cleared she would know where she was. The green numbers on the clock said 5 a.m. A street light shone through the window shade onto a patch of black and white rug. She studied the corners of the room, knowing that the shape on the couch was Paul. She felt safe, even though she knew there was something she should be worried about.

Then she remembered dreaming of an empty stateroom. She leaped from the bed and ran into Leelannee's room, stepping over the toys to reach the bed, thrashing for the child in the knot of covers. The child was breathing softly, her head dangling off the side of the bed. Jeanie moved her onto the pillow, gazing with rapture at her small, peaceful face. She draped the covers over her, tucking them close to the child's body. Then she sat on the edge of the bed, reliving rushes of horror and relief, astonished that somehow they were all back where they belonged.

Your wish is my command. She remembered saying that, with her own lips, with her own desire. Your wish is my dish. Was it possible? Could a part of her really want to give up her apartment, her neighborhood, her political work, for the easy surrender of the Church of All? If she hadn't been rescued . . . it was a humiliating thought. Maybe Eli Zinger would have let her walk out with Leelannee as he promised. Perhaps if the coalition hadn't moved so soon.

It was painful, sitting in the chill darkness with her memories rattling around in her mind. She couldn't bear it. Today would be a day like any other day, she decided. She would comfort herself and the child by keeping to their well-worn schedule.

She wandered back to the bedroom and stood over Paul, shaking him until he stirred. "Come on, baby, wake up. Don't we have to go to work today?"

Paul rubbed his eyes. "I don't know. Look on the refrigerator."

She stared at him for a moment, then remembered that indeed her schedule was taped to the refrigerator. She was due in at nine. "I don't work the early shift any more," she muttered. She peered into the half-empty refrigerator. There were gaps. Holes in the mind that she could fall through if she let go of the elusive present. She didn't remember Leelannee being that big. She didn't remember if she had settled with Eli Zinger.

Paul pulled on his pants and followed her into the kitchen. His hand was lifted to stroke her hair. "Are you okay?"

She pulled back gently. "No." He looked sad, so she added, "I will be."

"Will be what?"

"Okay." They both laughed. "I'm sorry I woke you, Paul, I don't have to be in until nine. What about you? You working today? We didn't set the alarm." We didn't. It was obvious. Part of her remembered they had set alarms together before. But she was afraid to let him touch and comfort her. She held herself taut for the next shock of memory that was breaking over her.

Paul pushed aside the curtain and looked out. The street lights flounced their wide skirts on the empty sidewalks. "I was going to skip work today. You should too. You need time to unravel."

The thought of unraveling scared her. What would she find when her brain started to work smoothly again. Who would she be? "I have to go to work. I got the rent due this week."

Paul shook his head slowly. "I think it's a bad idea for you to go to work. You started a big commotion yesterday. There are three people in jail. You had some kind of drug. I really think you need—"

"Don't tell me what I need! I need to go to work." She didn't like to be told what to do. Fall in left, right, left. Next he'd be telling her to nod her head and repeat after me.

Paul shrugged, looking out the window again. "Last night you couldn't even remember your name. Maybe you should see a doctor."

"Well, I remember now, I remember too much." She stepped onto one foot. "It's so cold in here, I'm going back to bed for an hour." She ran back to the bed and lay shivering for a few moments. When Paul passed on his way back to the couch she patted the mattress, motioning for him to join her.

He lay next to her, his arms folded across his chest, his elbows sticking out so she couldn't get near him. She wanted to approach him, but it took many minutes before she could emerge from her teeming brain. She sat up and studied him, trying to figure out if he was asleep. He opened one eye, saw her looking, and started to snore. She poked him in the ribs, laughing. "Come on, wake up, I need to talk to you."

He kept his eyes closed. "You don't need me. You just need to go to work."

"Yes, I need you."

"You don't need any advice. Your mind's all made up about everything. You got everything under control."

"Oh sure, sure." She pushed his arm up and wiggled her head onto his shoulder. He let his arm drop heavily around her. "Paul, do you think it will be safe to send Leelannee to school today?"

He squeezed her waist. "So you're all up to date now?"

"Yeah, I think so. Was I acting very weird yesterday?"

"You're acting weird today."

"That's why I just want to get back into the normal routine. I think it would be best for Leelannee to go to school and me to go to work and later on we can have . . . discussions or whatever. I can call the school and insist they don't release her to anyone but me. I'm the one who pays for that Zionist nursery, and I'm sure they've handled custody battles before. I probably should have done that yesterday instead of dropping Lee at Gail's."

"You didn't think they were that dangerous."

"No, I didn't."

"What do you think now?"

She shrugged. "What do you think?"

"I think they were trying to brainwash you."

"Oh, there's no such thing as brainwashing." She felt stiff with her head bent onto his shoulder, but she didn't want to move. The rest of the bed was cold.

"Meaning that of your own free will you wanted to stay there?"

"No, not exactly." The pressure in her head was building up and she saw spikes of light. "I can't talk about it. I don't . . . I want this to be like any other day."

"But it isn't."

"If I go to work . . . that should sober me up. Then later . . ."

He sighed and moved his hand around her bottom, letting her shift into a more comfortable position. "Let's get some more sleep." And he did fall asleep, breathing evenly and holding her in his arms where she kept craning her neck to see the clock that moved so slowly toward seven. She felt detached from herself. Her lips, her own lips, had said things she had never wanted to say. She had not settled with Eli Zinger. All the danger she put her child through, all the risks her friends took, were all worth nothing. She knew she couldn't have been drugged. She had been so careful not to eat or drink anything. She examined her arms for puncture marks, but there were none. A few minutes before seven, when the steam began to gurgle through the pipes, she got up and turned on the light. She took off her nightgown and examined the skin behind her knees and all the places they might have possibly stuck a needle. She couldn't find so much as a bruise.

She peered out the window for the first signs of dawn. Then she woke Leelannee, who sat up in bed promptly. "Is today school?"

"Yes. Do you want to go?"

"What day is it? Is it Friday? I'm supposed to light the candles this Friday."

"Okay, let's get you dressed." She searched Leelannee's drawers for clean clothes, assuring herself that lighting a few candles would not permanently damage the child. She had done her best to get Leelannee into a city daycare, but they were all full when she applied and by the time an opening came she had already enrolled her in the private school. She was glad in a way, proud that she was managing the payments.

Leelannee pulled her shirt on backward; then looked down wondering where the clown who decorated the shirt was. Jeanie laughed, tickling her, righting her clothes, tying her shoes, leading her into the bathroom to put toothpaste on the brush and watch that the child actually did brush her teeth and wash her face. Then she hurried into the kitchen to put the water to boil for hot wheat cereal. She wondered if Leelannee had eaten anything yesterday.

It was Leelannee who woke Paul up again, sitting on the edge of the bed and putting her face so close to his that he could feel her breathing. "I thought you were a mouse!" he said, pulling her into the bed and tossing her around.

"Let me go. Stop it. Ma, make him stop it."

"Do you want some hot cereal, Paul?"

"Sure, whatever you're making."

Jeanie made enough for all of them, and found herself eating cereal for the first time since she'd abandoned the gruel of the Church of All. "What about the Eddie Market show?" she said suddenly to Paul.

"I watched it last night, after you fell asleep."

"And?"

"I guess Gail and Justino went down and spoke to him. He described your case on the air."

"Oh. So there's still time. Did he talk about the government financing of All?"

"That's all he talked about. Jeanie, what exactly did they do to you in there? You should call him today and try and describe it. But maybe you should talk to Gail first. There are some people in jail . . . you have to get your stories straight."

"I'll see Gail at work."

They had both finished their cereal and Leelannee was still playing with her spoon. "Hurry. You'll miss the bus."

"Why don't you let me drive you?" Paul asked.

"Okay, great. Then I can go in and talk to the principal about—"

"You're going to talk to the principal?" Leelannee said. "I didn't go to his office. I didn't."

Jeanie waited until the child finished gulping her milk. "Why did you go to the principal's office?"

"Joshua pushed me."

"Oooh. Did you push him back?"

"No, I didn't push him back. I bited him."

Jeanie tried to bury her smile. "I don't want you biting."

Leelannee shook her head. "I'm a very nice girl, but I can bite harder than him."

Paul burst out laughing.

"Shh," Jeanie said. "Will you drive me to work too? Are you sure you want to take the day off?"

"After what happened on the dock the other day it's only right to leave the boss shorthanded."

Jeanie spent ten minutes looking for Leelannee's winter coat until she realized it must have been left at the Reverence Hotel. She piled her with sweaters and an older jacket with a button missing. She wrapped a muffler around the child's head and neck until she moved stiffly. Then Jeanie tossed on an old storm coat and hurried them out of the apartment. When they reached the elevator she heard the phone ringing in her apartment but decided to ignore it. She would call her parents on her break at work. She would call Eddie Market then too. She felt certain that a few hours at the cash register would straighten out her head.

As they came out of the elevator Jeanie saw the tower of Mrs. Feldman's magenta hair heading toward the laundry room. "I got it all set up," she yelled.

Jeanie peered around the corner. Gray webs of lint stretched from pipe to pipe. The floor was grimy with puddles waiting to catch dropped pieces of laundry.

"Is Tuesday night good for you?"

Jeanie nodded. Good for what?

"I called everyone on the steering committee. All of them except Mr. Grady can make it on Tuesday."

Fight where you are for what you need. She needed a cleaner laundry room. She was not burned out yet. She forced herself to meet Mrs. Feldman's eyes. "Tuesday's fine. What apartment?"

Another bout with the landlord, who hired too few workers to keep the building clean, who cried that being a landlord was most unprofitable, who threatened to move welfare families into the building. She would throw the marshal's keys down the sewer. Some things were clear enough.

25

The principal assured Jeanie that he could protect Leelannee, that she wouldn't be released to anyone but her mother. He didn't mention Leelannee biting Joshua, and Jeanie was careful not to inquire about it. She promised to come back sometime to discuss the Church of All with him, and was relieved to get out of his rabbinical study. She stopped to buy a newspaper before sliding into the white convertible next to Paul.

The story about Eli Zinger's alleged government connections was placed fairly prominently on the fifth page, alongside a photograph showing the bearded master with his arms raised in exhortation. His mystic power did not pulse through the newsprint. He might have been mistaken for a magician on a television talk show. The story said that attendance at tonight's Church of All rally was expected to be sparse.

"Does it say anything about that Senator's daughter?" Paul asked, as he navigated the traffic in the crowded Bronx streets.

Jeanie flipped through the pages to find the continuation of the story. "No. Nothing. You know I saw Helena Carpenter."

"We heard she was taken away in an ambulance last night."

"Well, I didn't do anything to her." Jeanie tossed the newspaper into the back seat. She stared at his profile. "I signed a paper asking for re-entry," she said softly.

"What?"

"They made me sign a paper. They said they'd take Leelannee to Vancouver."

Paul put his arm around her shoulder, pulling her closer. "It doesn't matter."

"No?"

"This is going to be done with soon, I hope."

"What do you think of my coalition friends now? It seems like you should be won over."

"They're okay. They sure risked their necks for you." The traffic was miraculously smooth on the Bronx River Parkway and Paul took it at high speeds.

"Not just for me. They want to expose the social role of the Church."

"You remember Justino riding that elevator?"

"No," she shrugged. It bothered her that there were still gaps. She would get the whole story from Gail at work.

"I hope that after today you're not going to need those people. Just give your testimony and be done with it."

"They might need us next time."

"Maybe we can take a few days' vacation later in the month. Do you ski?"

She leaned against him. "I'll still have plenty to do. The coalition is building for a big demonstration around the crisis. . . ."

"You're going to need a vacation. At least a couple of days of just worrying about me and Leelannee. That should be enough to keep your mind occupied."

"It's not enough."

"Hey, it's supposed to be enough." They were making Manhattan in record time, and it put both of them in good spirits.

"No," she laughed, "it will never be enough. I need company while I'm waiting for the tree to fruit. Look at this city. It could be so beautiful. . . ."

"It's beautiful in Vermont, right now."

Elation rose through her body like a fine spraying fountain. She was so used to dealing with temporary setbacks that she hardly knew how to accept this temporary triumph. She had, indeed, exposed Eli Zinger to unfavorable publicity. With any luck there'd be a congressional investigation. That would probably amount to little, she thought, but it would at least lose them a few followers and reverse their momentum.

She smiled over that until Paul pulled up in front of Mirrormart. "Are you really going in there?" he asked. "What am I supposed to do with the rest of my day?"

"Maybe I'll just work half a shift and say I'm sick. I want to pick Leelannee up from school myself."

"You want me to sit out front and wait for you?"

"No," she laughed. "Don't you have anything to do?"

"I could go downtown and pay the parking tickets I got yesterday."

"There you go."

"But where am I going to meet you?" They puzzled over that for a while, finally deciding that Paul would meet her for her 35-minute lunch break. She kissed him and jumped out of the car, running to the back entrance of Mirrormart to punch in on time.

A quick glance at the cards told her that both Gail and Justino were absent from work today. I shouldn't be so surprised, she told herself. I knew all along they put political work ahead of the job. But it bothered her as she dropped her card into the jaws of the time machine. She slipped into deep commitments to whatever she was doing, even a $3.25-an-hour job. She had to show up to feel that all was right with the world. Ah, maybe Gail and Justino were just late. They couldn't afford to take the chance of getting fired for cause.

She put her coat in the upstairs lockers that she, and a committee, had harassed the management into installing. The blue nylon smock, with its flared cut and big pockets, fit comfortably over her shirt. She was glad she'd traded her medium, which showed her bust but cut her under the arms, for a large that slumped off her shoulders but felt fine. A mirrorlike piece of plastic with JEANIE BURGER embossed on it was pinned over the embroidered pocket of her smock. There was no way to feel disconnected in such a smock.

She nodded to the other cashiers as she locked her cash drawer into the register. A row of customers quickly pushed their carts into her line. The glare of the supermarket lights reflected off the aluminum cases that lined the dozen aisles. For a moment she felt seasick, dizzy. She thought she was on the ferry leaving Nanaimo. She was worried about Leelannee. The expanse of the market was like a vast, buckling ocean.

The first customer had finished piling all her groceries on the counter and clicked her fingernails against the rail. "Cash or stamps?" Jeanie asked her.

"Cash!" the young brown-skinned woman said.

Jeanie began to ring up the groceries. She hated to ask about food stamps as much as the customers hated to hear it. Lines of faces quarreled with the question each day. How come you ask? Do you think I can afford to feed these kids without food stamps? Or, no, damn it, I don't qualify for stamps, that's why there's so little meat in the cart.

The customer opened brown paper bags and put them in her cart, starting to pack the heavier groceries at the bottom. Jeanie went through the motions of her job slowly. It took deliberation to keep her from slipping into another realm, to keep her from surrendering to her dizziness and swooning to the floor.

The next customer played the groceries back and forth over the line, trying to spend the exact amount of the stamps in her hand. Jeanie became absorbed in trying to help her, ringing several subtotals. The sounds of the large market filled her head. Manager's specials were being broadcast over the loudspeaker system. The other register women called out for prices, for more bags, for help in packing the groceries for the lines of customers that now reached halfway down the aisles. Jeanie began to pick up speed. She hit the keys with a quick, even pace, pressing the button to draw the line of groceries within her reach.

The manager stopped to bag some groceries so her line would speed up. "You still look sick. You look like you're gonna pass out."

Jeanie thought he was afraid she'd faint, hit her head on the counter, and collect disability for two years. "Yeah. I may have to go home early."

She pulled the items toward her very slowly until the manager got impatient and went to help another checker. Then she sped up. Once her rhythm was established she could turn to chat with the woman at the next register, who had just come back from a break. The woman said Gail and Justino had not showed up for work. Jeanie began to wonder how long she could last. She had counted on a hurried exchange with Gail. She was hoping for a few words to tell her it really wasn't terrible that she had signed up for re-entry, that she had surrendered again to Eli Zinger with her own lips, her own heart.

The morning was almost gone when Jeanie looked up from an order of thirty cartons of eggs. She found herself gazing into Eli Zinger's calm blue eyes. The sight refreshed her. A panorama of sky after the aluminum glare of the market. But a moment later the manager's voice came over the loudspeaker and she remembered where she was. Fear fell from her body like sheets of sweat. Did he have Leelannee again? She gazed around but the stockboys had disappeared and the girl at the next register was out to lunch. She saw that Eli had hung the CLOSED, PLEASE USE NEXT REGISTER sign and put up the chain behind his cart. She began to count the egg cartons again, checking to see if they were all extra-large.

"We're always misplacing you, Jeanette," he smiled. "You look so weary. Come, I will give you rest."

She kept her eyes on her shoes. She was just a dumb kid, she didn't know nuttin'. If you didn't answer them they would go away.

"Jeanette, don't be alarmed," Eli said. "I need you. We all need you. Our souls are crying out to each other."

He was attracting a few stares from the shoppers, who were drawn to his long white beard and religious garb.

Jeanie kept her eyes down on the egg cartons, feeling prickles on the back of her neck. "I gotta get back to work," she mumbled.

"The people who interrupted us yesterday were outsiders. They don't understand." His voice quaked and she looked up to see him raising his hands in front of his face. Oh, don't go into a trance here, Eli Zinger, they'll only sweep you out with the other damaged groceries. He held his face for a moment, then lowered his broad hands. "Don't let outsiders fill you with confusion and doubt, Jeanette. They woke your daughter in the middle of the night and dragged her out into the cold. They—"

She smacked her palm on the bell on top of her cash register, ringing for the manager. "Eli, I don't know what shit Dennis gave me yesterday, but it's all worn off."

"Come outside for a moment, Jeanette. We must reach an understanding. Cordite is mounting serious charges of breaking and entry, of hurting Helena Carpenter, of . . ."

Jeanie pressed the bags of eggs into Zinger's arms until he could barely balance. "I'm through with it, Eli. Get out of here. I don't want to see your face again."

He looked truly astonished and hurt. "Last night we were ready to soar together again. Don't you remember?"

"That's not all I remember." She glared at him, her shoulders held high in defiance.

He sighed. "God be with you, Jeanette."

She stared after him until he walked out of the automatic doors with the bags of eggs slipping toward his knees. She remained frozen in her position until the manager showed up.

"Who the hell was that?" the manager asked. "He looks like he thinks he can walk on water."

Jeanie shrugged. "He bought a lot of eggs. Look, Mr. Gorgiano, I'm sorry, I just don't feel well."

"So go home. Don't come in sick."

She nodded, waiting as they counted the money in the drawer and squared her sums. Then she walked slowly to the back of the store, checking to see if she had enough dimes. She called Leelannee's principal, who said there had been no disturbances. She called her mother at work, apologizing for not calling earlier, assuring her everything was fine. She called the loft and spoke to Gail, who shrieked when she heard that Jeanie was at work and quickly filled her in on the details of Eddie Market's investigation, the case being built against the arrested demonstrators, the importance of finally getting the original documents into Market's hands. Jeanie hung up the phone feeling elated. She had settled with Eli Zinger, but there was still plenty to do while she waited for the tree to fruit.

Her dizziness began to subside. She sat on the bench near her locker, her hands relaxed in the lap of her blue smock, feeling stronger and steadier than she had in years. She was something to contend with after all.

She glanced at her watch. It was still a bit early, but she had a hunch Paul was waiting. She took off her smock and put it in her locker. As she walked onto the street she noticed two men lounging by the Mirrormart window. She glanced at their shoes. They were streaked with dirt, unpolished. She smiled in relief, reminding herself that times had changed, that they didn't all wear black polished shoes now, that some wore white robes and beards and had faces like saints. Paul's car squealed to a halt in front of her.

"Ready for lunch?"

She got in the car, still smiling. "You have enough gas? We have three stops to make before we get Leelannee, and then—"

He groaned. "Did you see Gail?"

"No. She did what any smart person would do. She didn't come to work today. She's at the loft."

"How do you feel?"

Jeanie clutched her stomach, doubling over in mock pain. "When this is over we really got to take a vacation. First I want to sleep for a week. Then I want to watch TV for a week. . . ."

Paul moved the car slowly down the street. "Oh yeah? When's it going to be over?"

She narrowed her eyes, calculating. "It's difficult to say. Probably, it'll be over in a couple a hundred years."

A NOTE ON THE TYPE

The text of this book was set on the Linotype in Fairfield, the first typeface from the hand of the distinguished American artist and engraver Rudolph Ruzicka. In its structure Fairfield displays the sober and sane qualities of a master craftsman whose talent has long been dedicated to clarity. It is this trait that accounts for the trim grace and virility, the spirited design and sensitive balance of this original typeface.

Rudolph Ruzicka was born in Bohemia in 1883 and came to America in 1894. He has designed and illustrated many books and has created a considerable list of individual prints—wood engravings, line engravings on copper, aquatints.

Composed by The Maryland Linotype Composition Company, Inc., Baltimore, Maryland.
Printed and bound by The Haddon Craftsmen, Inc., Scranton, Pennsylvania.